KEEPING *Tessa*

KEEPING TESSA

Plump Playwright Act IV

Tessa du Toit's business trip is tainted by the discovery of her husband's infidelity. Deciding to go, to lose herself in London, she finds herself in a brawl and meeting the wealthy, sex-on-a-stick club owner, Camden Mathews.

Losing her heart wasn't the plan.

For Camden, Tessa's sexy accent and innocence beguile him as no other woman has. He pursues her, intent on sampling her lips for as long as she's in London. Until almost losing her cracks open his heart. He discovers he's in love, but to protect her, he must set her free.

Also by Sevannah Storm

The Blood of Legends Series
The Huntress
The Healer
*

The Gifting Series
Soul Forged
Fate Forged
Sun Forged
War Forged
Star Forged
Shadow Forged
Earth Forged
Lust Forged
Fire Forged
*

The Qaldreth Warriors
Sol Survivor
Dark Survivor (Coming soon)
*

The Space Hunter Chronicles
The Shikari

The Justisaar

*

Inkounter Series

Inkoded

*

Standalones

Xiaxan Fox

Ire of Silver

The Crucible of the Eternal

*

Plump Playwright Series

Plump Jane

Seducing Amelia

Loving Finley

Keeping Tessa

Kissing Navy

Acknowledgements

To my dearest, sweetest Londoner, Chris Pakes, for keeping me on the straight and narrow. Thank you for your guidance, your input, and your continued support. It means the world to me.

Sev

Chapter One

G*RAY SMOKE FILLED THE* pub while the traditional music and hum of chatting deafened Tessa. The vibe was boisterous, but it wasn't what she needed. She blinked to clear her vision, the smoke irritating her, itching her eyes. She sipped her soda, not a fan of warm beer or any beer, for that matter. Her colleagues had chosen this location, wanting to experience a London pub, and she'd been obligated to join them.

Framed photos and other bric-a-brac lined the walls, and the yellowed wooden ceiling had quaint stained-glass lighting.

She had other plans. A nightclub called to her, and when the taxi delivered them to the pub, electronic music reverberated down the road. There was one nearby, if she wanted to chance it. Sighing, she glanced at her dress. Not sure where they were going that evening, she'd overdressed. A navy blue figure-hugging satin dress, with a T-shirt collar trimmed in gold ribbon, clung to her plump breasts and too–wide hips, ending just above her knees.

Her braid fell over one shoulder. But despite her appearance pleasing her, the void in her heart threatened to swallow any joy. A white band marked her finger where, just a week ago, her wedding ring had resided. Brushing her negative thoughts aside, she shuffled along the leather booth in the pub.

"Just going for fresh air." She didn't wait for their responses.

Owen, one of her colleagues who knew her situation, arched a dark brow at her hasty exit. Checking her bank card and her room key were still in her hidden pockets, she strolled down the cobbled road toward the thump-thump of a nightclub. She walked with care since her steel-tipped navy stilettos slid on the stones. Not the best footwear to dance the night away, but the club loomed like a promised oasis.

On a brick wall, a glowing blue sign said 'Elysium.' Excitement gripped her, and she drew in a shuddering breath. The glass door was too narrow to be the main entrance, yet a hefty bouncer guarded it. His suit burst at the seams as it struggled to contain his bulk. Clasping his hands in front of him, he stared at her with an earpiece in his left ear, a little hidden by his carefree black locks.

"Good evening." She flashed him a smile.

Kindness cost her nothing, whether she had a reason to smile or not. He nodded in greeting. She drew in another deep breath, hoping to calm the fluttering in her chest, and peered up the stairs behind him. Faced with the lure of vibrating music and losing herself in the rhythm, she hesitated. What was she doing? She was forty-four years old and didn't belong here.

"Are you all right, ma'am?"

She met his concerned expression to give him a shaky laugh. Ma'am? That said it all. "I'm fine, thanks. Just not sure if I should be here, y'know."

"Why not?"

"Too old, I guess. I haven't danced in years." There it was. At least she'd been honest.

He ran his gaze over her. Stay-up stockings hid her varicose veins, the dress hid her cesarean scars, but other than that, she was in good condition, surprising after losing sixty pounds. She still had more to lose and would never be slender, but at her age, she was content with having some sort of waist.

"You're never too old to dance," he said with a chuckle, revealing a dimple in his cheek.

She laughed, appreciating his kindness, and thrust out her hand. "My name's Tessa du Toit."

"Bart," he said and unfolded his arms to shake her hand with his meaty one. "Where are you from? Your accent is beautiful."

"South Africa. I'm here for a conference."

"And to dance." He wiggled his eyebrows.

"Maybe not," she said with a self-deprecating chuckle.

Raucous laughter preceded three men who stumbled toward them. The stench of alcohol reached her before one man drew to a halt. His blue-tipped hair stood up like he'd stuck his fingers in a socket.

"Go home." Bart folded his arms across his barrel chest. He seemed to grow taller, more intimidating.

"Who are you to stop me?" Blue-tipped asked, shoving his face at Bart, even though he had to do so on his tippy-toes.

"Yeah, what you gonna do?" another man said, his words barely discernible.

His jacket hung at an angle, which might have been a stylistic choice. The third man mumbled and nodded, his gaze shifting from side-to-side, while he rubbed his soul patch with dirty fingers.

Bart lowered an arm to usher her behind him, protecting her. She glanced around him in time to see the light reflect off a silver blade. Her focus flew to the three men to assess their stances. Soul-patch had also drawn a blade. He lunged toward Bart, and she hip-nudged the bouncer out of the way of an upward stab—the oriental. Grabbing Bart's forearm for leverage, she side-kicked Blue-tip. Her foot connected with his chest, imprinting his T-shirt with her shoe and the square of her heel. He flew backward. Fire burned along the back of her thigh, but she thought nothing of it when pulling muscles was normal for her.

His cohorts blinked at their fallen friend clutching his bleeding chest. Bart punched Soul-patch, who'd tried to stab him, knocking him out. She expected it from a man with his fist size. Jacket-man thrust his dagger at her, and she redirected his strike, gripping his wrist between her underarm and chest, then twisted her body, forcing him to drop the weapon. It clattered to the floor, but she didn't search for it. She grabbed him behind the neck, yanked him toward her, and kneed him twice in the groin before striking him on the nape of his neck. Gripping his groin, he crumpled to the floor and hollered like a dying man.

With her fists raised to protect her head, she scanned the defeated attackers, checking over her shoulder in case they had friends. A flickering light illuminated the stairs through the glass door, but no one waited to attack. She faced Bart and gasped, lowering her fists. Blood stained his white T-shirt, now visible since he'd wrenched his jacket to the side to assess his wound.

"That's a lot of blood." She swatted his hand away to peel up his shirt. The shallow wound bled freely. She scrunched the fabric and held it to his torso. "Direct pressure," she said. "Let's get you to a hospital."

"Not necessary. Marc's quite good at patching us up." He pressed a finger to his earpiece. "Send the rookie and tell Marc, I'm..." Bart glanced at her. "That *we're* coming, and call the clean-up crew."

Within a minute, an athletic young man bounded down the stairs in the same outfit as Bart, sans beefiness.

"Come." Bart held out his hand, ignoring the questions the rookie fired at him the moment he opened the door.

She hesitated, but the look in Bart's brown eyes implied he would wait all night for her. Shooting a glance at his wound, she slid her hand in his.

The air inside the club was oppressive, but the music was a siren-call. When Bart spoke to another bouncer, she swayed her hips with her heart mirroring the beat's hypnotic pulse. Bodies writhed on the dance floor, and blue lighting cast an eerie glow over the décor. Bart tugged on her hand, and they meandered through the crowds to a black door nestled behind the back-bar. He dragged her up more stairs until they spilled into an office.

A mahogany desk rested to the rear of the room. Glass walls showed off the nightclub below, and bulky leather couches consumed the remainder of the space. The door closed behind her, and the thump-thump formed muted background noise.

Alone with a stranger, she stiffened.

When he released her hand and smiled, she relaxed. Bart was a big ol' teddy bear.

Chapter Two

"WHAT THE FUCK HAPPENED?" A dark-haired man burst forward, casting a dismissive glance at Tessa like she was a floozy. It made her chuckle. Married for twenty years, her days of flooziness were long behind her. Though, one look at the man, and she might consider dusting off those forgotten skills. Jeans hugged powerful thighs, the kind she drooled over in class. A button-up blue shirt draped over broad shoulders, and he wore a scowl like a professional. Aware she should be scared, now alone with *two* strangers, she couldn't drum the energy to find either man intimidating.

"Three men with knives. Watch the security feed, Marc." Bart dropped onto the three-seater couch. "But do that later. This hurts like hell."

"Fine. Who's the woman?" Marc grabbed a medkit from a cupboard.

"Marc, this is Tessa. Honey, say hello, tell him where you're from, and how long I've known you. Put his unfounded fears at ease."

"Hello, Marc. I'm from South Africa, and I've known Bart for oh, say...ten minutes."

Marc halted mid-stride. "Your accent is sex-on-a-stick." He blinked at her.

Heat splashed across her cheeks. "So I've heard. Could you take care of Bart, please? His wound is seeping blood."

Marc flicked the box open. While he worked, she strolled over to the glass wall. The crowds danced with abandonment, and she wished she could join them, to allow no thoughts to dampen her spirits. The beat thumped up through her heels, tempting her to throw caution to the wind, her hands in the air, and her hips from side-to-side.

"Go downstairs and dance, luv. You know you want to," Bart said, then hissed, glaring at Marc.

She sighed. "I'm tempted, but I think this is as close as I'll get."

"Do you realize your dress is torn, and there's blood streaking the back of your thigh?" Marc gestured with a bloodied gauze.

Groaning, she rested her burning cheek to the cool glass. *Holy cow!* She'd flashed these poor bastards. Wait... What? She twisted and scowled, only now acknowledging the stinging fire streaking her thigh.

"He must have cut me when I kicked him." She grimaced, replaying the fight in her mind, one strike at a time.

"Here, painkillers." Marc wiped his blood-stained hands on a cloth. He bounded forward, gathered her palm in his, and shook two capsules onto it.

She nodded her thanks, though not planning on swallowing pills from a stranger. Thankfully, Marc shoved off, not wanting for her to swallow and stick out her tongue for him to check she had. She slipped them into a hidden pocket and studied Bart with his shirt off. Muscles carved in umber had her smiling. Intricate tattoos marred their dark landscape. No doubt, each with their story.

A tat peeked out from under Marc's shirt collar, leaving her to guess what it was. Something Celtic, a naked woman, his mother's name. She'd never find out.

The patch over Bart's wound looked professional. He grunted when he rose off the couch to take a shirt out of the wall of cupboards opposite the glass. Judging by the stack inside, they kept stock for a reason.

When she focused on Marc again, he was sitting behind the desk, drying his hands on another towel. The scent of soap had her searching the office for a basin. There was one tucked into a narrow alcove with a bar fridge below it. Bart paused beside her, pulling on his jacket, while Marc watched something on a monitor on the desk. She did up Bart's buttons before smoothing his lapels, standing on her tippy-toes to reach.

"Tessa, your heel sank into his chest." Marc applauded as if seeing her do so pleased him. Bouncing in his chair, he resembled a little boy watching wrestling.

She chuckled. "That wasn't my intention. I had to create distance between the oriental stab and Bart."

"Oriental?" Marc arched a brow. "Bart, I'll send Doc to find you when he gets in."

Bart swallowed his painkillers sans water. "Come see me before you leave, Tess."

She waved. "I promise."

"I'll tend to her wound and call a taxi for her," Marc said, to which Bart nodded, opened the door releasing the dampened electronic music before closing it behind him. "On the couch with you."

"What?" Her face burned cold, and she struggled to swallow, not trusting her thoughts. Like a handsome man would show interest in her. "On my stomach?"

She marched across, hoping to portray a level of confidence she was far from feeling. Sprawling on the cold leather, she kept her heels up so they wouldn't scratch the couch, then rested her chin on the armrest, throwing her arms over it, as well.

"Your dress is ruined. Stockings too."

"One hell of a party." She chuckled. Silence met her response, but she didn't look at him, preferring to wallow in her embarrassment. Dancing was all she'd wanted, not whatever this was.

"Fuck, your accent is sexy."

Like she hadn't heard that before. "Take a recording. It'll last longer." She was joking, but his gentle touch stilled, and a moment later, he thrust his phone in her face. "Okay." She grabbed it. "Wake up call?"

"Yeah, that sounds good."

"Good morning, sleepyhead, rise, and shine. So many things to see, too many women to do. Up you get, sweetheart. Time waits for no man, not even your sexy ass." She hit the end button and held the phone to him. Once again, his fingers stilled. With her hands free, she returned them to the armrest. "Is it deep? Do I need stitches?"

The thought of a trip to the hospital made her grumble. Twelve hours on a plane wouldn't help her wound, and how the hell would she explain this when she got home? Her sensei would love to hear about it though, giggling at her and asking her to re-enact it. If anyone had a naughty face, it was the man who taught her how to maim.

"If you do, we'll ask Doc to do it," Marc said.

"If?" The wound must be bleeding so much he couldn't see how deep it was.

"I haven't had a look at it yet, what with tearing your stockings and wiping up the blood."

"What the fuck is going on? I have the clean-up crew downstairs, and the rookie's working with Bart. Up here, you have a tart on the couch."

She jerked at the booming voice, then again when he slammed the door shut.

"Relax, boss, watch the feed first," Marc said, but there was humor in his voice, not taking the man's fury seriously.

"Do you bring tarts here often?" She kept her voice low. The back of the couch was too high to see over, but the owner of that raspy voice sounded lethal.

"You're not a tart, Tessa." Marc patted her shoulder and probably smeared blood on her satin dress.

She frowned, lamenting the total failure of her nightclub adventure.

The stranger strode past her head, and she watched him slip around his desk to drop into the chair. Her breath caught, and she looked away, hoping he hadn't heard her reaction. Wheat-colored hair cascaded over his Adonis features. His hair looked tousled and too long where it brushed the collar of his steel-blue tailored jacket. Broad shoulders and solid biceps threatened to split the seams. Just like Bart's. His angular jaw was squarish, drawing attention to his pursed lips. She opted not to catalog his features further. Her old heart wouldn't survive it.

"The timing's too perfect." Boss leveled his blue gaze on her.

Distrust came off him in waves, mingling with an intensity of power. Was it his sex appeal? She couldn't say, not without staring. His words settled in her dazed mind, and she laughed, not caring if she offended him. He thought she'd choreographed everything. A mother of two mistaken for a spy?

"Lie still." Marc gripped her calve.

"Listen, boss." She shook her head at the absurdity of this situation. "I don't know who you are, and I don't give a rat's ass about whatever you're doing that involves espionage. I'm going to take a taxi, drink Marc's painkillers, and forget this entire evening ever happened."

"You're not from here." Boss's statement had her rolling her eyes. He was next-level genius.

"Bingo." She rested her forehead on the armrest as exhaustion beat at her. "If I don't need stitches, I'd like to go now."

"Does she?" Boss's voice was closer, and she tilted her head to look at him.

With him looming over her, his proximity had her heart fluttering in her chest like trapped flying ants. Their falling wings pooled in the pit of her stomach, drawing forth a different kind of heat. She didn't find him devastating, attractive, intimidating, or sexy. She didn't, but her pinging hormones screamed otherwise. *Shit.*

"I'll call Doc to come in early. He can check on Bart, too." Marc leaned back on his haunches and pressed his phone to his ear.

"Then return to your post. I'll take care of our angel," Boss said.

"Angel?" She snorted. "Whatever, dude."

"Dude?" He sounded a little stunned, but she wasn't going to stare at him again, not when it had her heart doing the rumba. At least, a part of her got to dance tonight.

"Yes, it's that or Boss." She gave him a pointed look as if to say, 'pick one.'

"The name's Camden Mathews."

She cursed the fates for his lovely name.

Marc held out his hand to her, and she accepted it for a shake. "Tessa, sweetheart, it's been a *pleasure* from my side." He flashed her a charming smile before jogging out of the office and leaving her alone with Cam.

Panic struck, and she pushed herself off the couch, balancing on her knees. She'd rather scramble off the couch, bleed in the taxi, and make her escape. Anything but be alone with him. Sanity returned, and despite the urge to bolt gripping her, she doubted she could reach the door before he stopped her. She didn't want him touching her. Just the thought of his hands on her spiked her temperature and snatched her breath. Trembling, she sank onto the couch. Maybe the knife tip held poison? That was a preferable explanation for her feverish longing.

"Your dress is ruined," he said, having removed his jacket and rolled up his sleeves on sculpted arms entwined with tattoos. The crisp white shirt gaped at the base of his throat and clung to a chest screaming for a good licking. More tats peeked out. He kneeled alongside the couch, bringing his spicy cologne closer. "Your red-lace boy shorts are showing."

Tingles rushed down her throat, and she groaned, turning away from him. Yes, she had worn her best lingerie—red-lace boy shorts with a black bustier—hoping to boost her confidence. That they didn't match didn't matter to her since no one was supposed to see her in them. At least, she had worn panties since she usually went commando, but this dress was inches shorter than her normal style. Shivering at the thought of her naked ass exposed, she sighed, grateful she was decently covered. He stroked something cool along her wound, shooting shards of heated agony up her thigh. She settled in for the wait, her lips pinched to stifle a gasp.

"So, where are you from?"

"Africa," she said. "I wanted to dance tonight, to lose a piece of myself in London." She drew in a shuddering breath, fighting the sting of tears behind her eyes. Ruined dress and evening, she wasn't about to add ruined makeup to the list.

"You still can." His voice rubbed along her senses, and she shook her head. No to the evening, to the dancing, to losing herself, to the effect of this man on her body. Just...no.

"Every man here thinks I'm a woman of loose morals. I'm tempted to search your couch cushions for random bits of underwear."

"You do look like a cougar." He chuckled, husky, deep, and evocative.

She squeezed her eyes shut but was unable to cover her ears or calm her erratic heartbeat. "Huh. I'm not showing cleavage, and the only reason you're seeing a bit of my thigh is that I tore my dress doing a side kick."

His fingers stroked said thigh, and she quivered. She didn't think he'd done it on purpose, especially when something cold dabbed at her wound again.

"I'm here, boss." A man burst into the office accompanied by a woman's wailing cry and the thump of a new beat.

"Good, Doc. Does she need stitches?"

She forced herself to relax when she sensed movement, assuming Cam had risen to his feet to allow the doctor access.

"Who's the tart?"

"Fuck," she whispered. The doctor had proven her point.

"She's my guest, Doc, and I'd appreciate a little respect." Cam's voice had hardened with steel, but he'd forgotten he'd called her a tart not ten minutes ago. She decided against pointing that out. The quicker the doctor looked at her leg, the sooner she could leave. If she went to the hospital, the fee would be astronomical and beyond her ability to pay.

"Sorry, ma'am," the doctor said.

Ma'am? Sensing she was on the verge of tears, she smothered a giggle. She was made of sterner stuff, dammit. Two caesareans, for pity's sake.

"I'll inject you then stitch you up. I'll just use a little anesthetic. I don't want you to lose the use of your leg for the next twelve hours."

"Appreciate it." Despite her casual response, she didn't like the sound of that. Inject her with what? Panic gripped her, coiling tendrils of fear in her stomach as she imagined all sorts of horrors, ending with her lying in a tub of ice minus a few organs. "Listen, this is all unnecessary. I'll just have Owen look at it."

Cam dropped to his haunches in front of her and clasped her face between his long-fingered hands. His citrus cologne with a hint of antiseptic engulfed her. "Tessa, please, trust me to help you."

His touch burned her, sending shards of electricity sliding down her neck toward her nipples. Holy shit, this man was intense. His blue gaze pierced hers, and she didn't doubt his sincerity. Forced to face him meant she had to admit he was the perfect example of manhood she'd seen in a while.

Having stared at him for who knew how long, she blurted, "Okay, I place my life in your hands, Cam."

The dimpled smile he blessed her with had her grumbling again. She had to survive tonight, then she need never endure this level of sex appeal again.

"Scared of needles?" He laced his fingers through hers, his palm rougher than expected.

She shook her head and lay still, letting the doctor do his thing. The injection pinched, the liquid burned, then the back of her thigh numbed. Okay, one thing they hadn't lied about. She wiggled her toes, proving the numbness went no farther than promised.

Cam continued to hold her hand and distracted her by stroking his thumb across her knuckles. There was nothing else to focus on but his handsome features. Gray brushed his temples, so he wasn't as young as she'd thought. He vibrated with life—an energy as seductive as the music's drumbeat. A glance at his eyes found him watching her. For the life of her, she couldn't prevent the heat from staining her cheeks.

"Done, twelve stitches, and I've dressed it. The bandage will need daily replacement.

"Thanks, Doc." She squeezed Cam's hand before releasing it and him from his promise to help her.

He rose to his feet to discuss something with Doc in hushed tones, and a minute later, the doctor left. She reverse-sprawled herself, uncaring that she shoved her backside in the air. This way, she wouldn't pull on her stitches. Standing, testing her weight on her leg, she released a deep breath when it held firm.

"Thank you for taking care of me. I should head to the hotel. Tomorrow's the last day of the conference."

"You don't know who I am?" He leaned his backside on his desk and crossed his long legs at the ankles. His dark jeans coated his muscled legs, and she bit her bottom lip. Wow, just...wow. He cupped the desk's wooden edge, wrapping his fingers around it.

A moment later, she swallowed past the lump in her throat and hurried to answer him. "I do." He stiffened. "You're Boss, Camden Mathews. As to who you are in London or Europe or wherever, sorry, no idea. Africa's a little disjointed from the rest of the world."

Her words must have calmed him since his shoulders relaxed a little, and a smirk teased his lush lips. "Can I get you anything before you go?"

He gestured to the rolls of bandages the doctor had left her and a bottle of what she suspected were painkillers. She had Marc's pills for later and her own stashed in her luggage.

"A copy of tonight's music if it's possible. I've liked every mix I've heard so far."

Her request surprised him, arching his brow. His grin revealed a dimple in his left cheek. That was mean of him. She wasn't at her best nor strongest if a dimple could disarm her with such ease.

"Done, and I'll have my driver take you. It's the least I can do."

She stepped to the door with care. He followed her, not pressurizing her to hurry. She didn't want to tumble down the stairs since it was known to happen to her often. With his hand at the base of her spine, he escorted her to the front entrance.

"Wait, I promised Bart I'd say goodbye." She had to spin into him to yell in his ear.

He slipped his arms around her, holding her against him until the granite hardness of his body warmed hers. She ceased to breathe, peering at his face while waiting for his response. With her body registering his strength and darts of need siphoning her ability to resist him, she almost sank into his embrace. His expression was a blurred mixture of surprise, appreciation, and confusion. The reasons behind any of those emotions darkening his eyes were unfathomable under the circumstances.

He dug his fingers into the flesh of her hips before nodding, spinning her away from him as if she weighed nothing. He steered her to Marc instead, spoke to him then escorted her toward the entrance.

She waved farewell to Marc, and as they burst into the crisp air, Bart waited for her. He pulled her into his arms for a crushing hug, engulfing her in muscle and cologne, smashing her nose into his chest. She chuckled, and he released her, setting her back on her feet.

"Farewell, Tess-luv, and thanks for saving me."

She patted him on a bicep and tried to hide her sadness. Getting to know him better would have been a gift. "Have a good life, Bart, for me." Blinking back tears, she hurried to Cam, who held a door open to a fancy black Merc.

"Anthony will take you to your hotel, and I'm sorry for my 'tart' comment." His hesitation implied he didn't often apologize.

"I should take it as a compliment." She shrugged at the strangeness of the evening.

"Good night, Ms. Tessa."

"Good night and farewell, Mr. Camden." She slid into the car, careful to lift her thigh when doing so. Buckling herself in, she waved goodbye to him. Only then did he close the door and thump the roof of the car. Holy crap, that wasn't what she'd planned when she left her colleagues at the pub.

She stared out the window unseeingly, too dazed by the night's events to take note of the passing scenery despite a fleeting glimpse of the Gherkin. The ride was swift, and Anthony, the driver, dropped her outside her hotel.

It was late; few guests hovered in the foyer, and she drew the eyes of those still present. Hobbling into the elevator, she pressed her floor number and slumped against the mirrored side. She didn't glance at her reflection, not wanting to know how awful she looked. Sometimes ignorance was preferable. She paused outside Owen's room, considered waking him, then decided against it.

In her room, her phone had missed calls from Owen and her husband. She messaged Owen she was fine and back in her room but chose not to respond to Forest. After what he'd done for the past six months, she wanted nothing to do with him. Not wanting to get the dressing wet, she chose not to shower. Instead, she researched the name on Marc's pills before popping them. She removed her makeup, brushed her teeth then slipped into her baggy T-shirt and between the bed's crisp sheets.

One day, she'd look back on tonight with a laugh, but for now, the image of Cam's blue eyes haunted her. Within moments, sleep dragged her down, a side effect of her usual reaction to painkillers. The sluggishness would grant her peace from reliving the night's events and analyzing every expression that crossed Cam's handsome face.

Chapter Three

CAM STARED AT THE couch where Tessa had spent her time. If he closed his eyes, he could remember her sprawled there, her heels up to protect his furniture. He'd realized that when she carefully climbed off the couch post-stitches. What sort of woman was considerate of his leather? The foreign kind, apparently.

Her words were sassy in that sexy, husky-yet-sweet voice of hers. Her accent had stroked over him like silken caresses. *Tessa.* Everything she'd said last night was true. She'd flown in from Johannesburg, South Africa to attend a conference, verified by Anthony last night.

Cam awaited the full report on her background check. For now, he relived their meeting. The copper-red color of her hair against the blue of her dress. The smoothness of her inner thigh. The flash of red contrasting with her demure outfit. She had grumpy Bart fawning all over her and made a champion in Marc.

If she was a spy, she was a damned good one.

"You're here early." Marc strolled into the office, flicking his damp hair off his temple.

"I tasked Watts to investigate our little angel." Cam thrummed his fingers on his desk, willing the phone to ring.

"Ah, still distrusting." Marc shook his head.

Cam flattened his palm on the desk. "You don't suspect foul play?"

"Hell, no. Tessa's a sweetheart. She didn't snoop when I tended to Bart, didn't ask any business questions, and as far as I could tell, just longed to dance. She's been hurt recently if you want my professional opinion. The pain lingers in her brown eyes."

"Yeah, I saw that too. She was close to tears at one point." Cam grimaced, remembering the spike of pain lancing through him at the shimmer in her eyes. She'd tried to hide the tears from him. A spy might have used them to manipulate.

The desk phone rang, and he picked it up before the second ring. Hearing Watts on the other end, he activated the speakerphone and returned the handset to its cradle.

"She's legit." Watts's voice was muffled as he chewed. "Mother of two, married, and attending a conference here in London."

Ice drenched Cam's loins... Married, not available, not single... Not interested. She hadn't smiled in a flirting manner, hadn't sought any excuse to touch him except on the dance floor. That had been a necessity, but he hadn't resisted tugging her closer to press her lush breasts against his chest. Not by an arched eyebrow or a delicate smirk did she show interest.

"Married? She wasn't wearing a wedding ring." Marc sat on the edge of the couch, resting his elbows on his knees.

Watts cleared his throat. "I hacked her correspondence; seems husband cheated on her with some tart."

Cam winced. The irony wasn't lost on him. "She wanted to lose herself in London," he said to the room in general. "What's her itinerary?" He flicked his gaze at his Rolex and grunted—almost teatime.

Watts typed on something as he accessed the data. "London for two more days, but her return flight is booked eight days from now."

"Odd." Cam arched a brow as if to say I-told-you-so.

"Not really. She's spending time with two sets of friends and visiting a few publishers. I trawled her social media, and there's nothing, but under her pseudonym, she's quite popular. Writes romance. The short story I read was rather good. Damn near split my jeans." Watts chuckled, but Cam squashed that imagery before it formed.

It was Marc's turn to arch a brow for an I-told-you-so. "Anything else unusual?"

Watts's slurped a beverage. "Nope, she's clean from my perspective. What's your issue with her, boss?"

"A mother of two took down two knife-wielding men from the Sorora syndicate, Watts." Cam rubbed his face and tapped the keyboard to replay the feed from last night.

"I can explain that. She's done Krav Maga for three years." Something played in the background as if Watts watched a video, too.

"She said oriental stab." Marc nodded with a pleased-with-himself expression.

"Thanks, Watts. Expect the usual payment." Cam hung up the call and watched Tessa knee the man on the security feed.

"What fascinates you?" Marc darted behind him to watch, adding sound effects when he reacted to each punch or kick.

"Everything. There wasn't any deception. What you see is who she is." He found it refreshing not to be on his guard with her. She hadn't thrown herself at him, hadn't seen him as an endless well of money. She had looked at him as a human being, someone worthy of knowing.

"You've had prettier." Marc's words solidified Cam's decision, in his chest and mind. He had every intention of seeing her again.

"True, but all of them wanted something from me. When I offered to get her anything, she asked for a copy of the club's playlist."

"She's genuine. I liked that about her. That and her sexy accent. If I could bottle it..." Marc chuckled. "Oh, but I have the next best thing." He flipped out his phone, and her voice played.

The lust punching through Cam had him shifting in his chair as he tried to ease the growing ache in his groin. "Fuck." He picked up his phone and dialed Watts. "Find out if her husband's still cheating on her." He called Anthony next.

"Off to woo her?" Marc frowned. "Just don't break her heart, Cam."

"Her playlist, bandages, and dinner." Cam scowled at having to justify himself to anyone.

"It's not yet teatime. Isn't she in mid-conference?"

"Send me that voice recording." Cam gathered the bandages in one hand, slid the memory stick in his back pocket, then bounded down the stairs. Eagerness energized him, rushing him across the lit nightclub to the waiting car.

"Tessa," he said by way of instruction, shuffling along the backseat and placing his backside in the exact spot she'd sat last night.

He grabbed the seatbelt and sniffed it, picking up a hint of her perfume. It wasn't overly sweet or heady. Just like her. What the hell was he doing? She showed no interest in him last night, and yet, he couldn't stop thinking about her. He analyzed every word she'd spoken, the angle of her head, and those expressive brown eyes.

By the time the car stopped, he hadn't thought of a plan of approach. He climbed out, not waiting for Anthony to open the door, then strolled into the foyer. The staff burst into a flurry. At least they knew who he was. The manager rushed toward him, smoothing his hair back as if the neatness of it mattered.

"Mr. Mathews, what an honor. How can I be of assistance?" Perspiration beaded the man's upper lip. Yes, they had a right to fear him, but really, why would he kill random hotel personnel?

"A lady was injured at my club last night. I need to find her." He arched a pointed brow and waited.

The man jerked then rushed to the front desk. Cam trailed him, wanting to hear everything discussed.

"Tessa du Toit asked for a bandage this morning, Mr. Mathews." The manager dipped his head like Cam was royalty.

"Where is she now?" Impatience erupted his emotions, and he tightened his control, his pinched lips revealing his inner struggle.

"In a conference room." The manager gestured to a door. "They break for tea in ten minutes, Shall I escort you to the venue?"

When Cam nodded, the man barreled ahead, leading him down a wide passage to a small room. The catering staff had placed food platters on the table alongside freshly brewed coffee. He dismissed the manager with a nod and approached the windows facing the hotel's atrium, prepared to practice his non-existent patience. He couldn't recall when he had last waited for a woman. Except for his sister, but promptness wasn't in Selena's vocabulary. Talking and laughing preceded the crowd exiting the conference room, but the moment Tessa walked in, his focus sharpened.

What she wore snatched his breath. A deep-blue pinstriped knee-length skirt hugged her curves with a wide corset-like leather belt cinching her waist from hips to under her breasts, thrusting them up. A crisp white shirt stretched over her ample breasts. Brown peep-toed shoes finished a beautiful outfit. Her hair was loose, brushing her shoulders and curling down her back. Today she wore bold-red lipstick. The sight of it made him want to nibble it off. What underwear was she wearing? He was eager to find out.

When she saw him, her lips curled into a delighted smile lacking pretense. As she hurried toward him, he couldn't miss her sculpted calves, something he hadn't admired yesterday when he'd had the chance. Earned from her martial arts training, no doubt.

Her scent surrounded him, and he drew in a slow breath, relishing the spiciness of it.

"Cam, what are you doing here?"

He hid the shiver her voice inspired. "Bandages, music, and a thank-you dinner."

"Thank you?" She arched a brow in surprise.

"For saving Bart." Cam raised his chin. The excuse was lame, but he was stumped as to how he could persuade her to dine with him. Most women pursued him. He couldn't recall the last time he'd done the asking.

Her eyes widened, as did her smile. "Unnecessary, but I'd love dinner." Her lips twisted as she sighed. "I don't eat after three, but I'll keep you company. I'll be a cheap date." Color flooded her cheeks, and she lowered her gaze. "I didn't mean date-date."

Her embarrassment had him laughing with the warmth in his chest unexpected. And he'd thought her a spy? "How much longer before I can whisk you away?"

"Now?" She gasped and glanced around. "We're wrapping up. I'll ask Owen to pack up my laptop. Give me a minute."

She rushed off, her short steps swaying her ass until she paused in front of a tall, dark-haired man in jeans. He greeted her, looked at Cam, then frowned. Not once was his gaze admiring, and the glint of gold on his wedding finger explained why. As she zigzagged back to Cam, she didn't notice the appreciative glances from the other men present. He fought the urge to glare them into showing her respect. The few men he did frown at, hastily looked away.

"I'm ready; do I need to bring anything?" Her fingers twitched like she missed carrying something.

"No, just you is perfect." He placed his hand at the base of her spine, deciding he didn't like the leather belt. Last night, he'd relished the heat of her through her dress. He ushered her into his car, waiting for her to slide across before slipping in next to her.

"The usual, Anthony," he said and twisted on the seat to look at her. "How's your wound?"

"Good. The hotel's nurse-on-staff bandaged it this morning."

Relief flooded him, and he found himself nodding. "It doesn't look like it hinders your movement."

"I can't sit for prolonged periods, and I have mild painkillers that help without making me drowsy." She smoothed her skirt with the palms of her hands, a sign of her nervousness. "You don't have to take me to dinner. I didn't do anything Bart couldn't handle on his own. I might've made it worse for him. He's okay, right?" Her brow furrowed, and as he studied her upturned face, he marveled at her sincerity.

"He's doing well, and to hear him tell it, you're his guardian angel," Cam lied with ease. He hadn't spoken to Bart, but the way the man had looked upon her hinted at a light infatuation.

She chuckled, flicking a wrist and dismissing Bart's admiration. "And Marc?"

"He's well. I hear you're a writer."

She gasped then chuckled, the sound enchanting. "You had me investigated? I sure as hell didn't mention that to anyone last night. Only Owen knows."

"The investigator thought your short story was good," Cam said, prepared to be honest with her on this. She laughed, and her brown eyes sparkled to life. He liked the look of it. "What's your nom-de-plume?"

"Elisa Dawn," she said.

He whipped out his phone and navigated to his eBook app, typing in the name with his thumbs. She had written over twelve books; the covers were stunning—creative, unique, and action-packed. He bought them all.

"Did you find them?" Her gaze traveled his face, her white teeth dimpling her bottom lip.

"Yes." He tucked his phone away and grinned. "Sexy stories saved for bedtime," he said. A fresh pink climbed her throat. He longed to trace its path with his lips. "Which ones should I read, and which ones should I not touch?"

"It depends on your preferred genre. Mystic Sails is a no-no. It's one of my first ones, and I've come a long way since then."

He nodded like he considered her guidance with due diligence when he had every intention of reading that one first.

"I'd recommend you read the samples before buying any. Besides, if you want to read one, I'll send you a free copy."

Yet another sign she didn't want anything from him. Any businesswoman worth her salt would've urged him to buy all her novels. Tessa was a soft-hearted woman who loved to write—earning an income from it wasn't what drove her.

Outside his favorite restaurant, he ushered her inside, still hating the feel of the leather instead of her supple skin beneath her shirt. He slid into his usual table, enjoying the soft candlelight flickering across her features. It drew his gaze to her lips. She didn't have the perfect plumpness he preferred. Regardless, her lips were sexy with a tiny scar under her bottom lip, dimpling it.

"A sparkling water, please," she said to Cam when the waiter hovered.

He placed the order and settled in. Resting his elbows on the edge of the table, he steepled his fingers. "Why don't you eat dinner?"

"I used to be the size of a house." She chuckled. "Now I eat one massive bowl of salad a day, and that's it. Don't lecture me about the importance of breakfast or three meals a day. My skinny self is proof it's a lie." She toyed with the napkin before draping it across her lap. "It's been tough, though, being here. No exercise, no copious amounts of salad. And the breakfast coffee smells so good." Her gaze drifted, then she chuckled, her attention returning to him with a jolt. "Are you famous or something?" she asked in a stage whisper. "Every woman here is hating me right now."

He glanced around the restaurant, seeing the many feminine gazes for the first time, then released a deep sigh. "Just rich," he said.

"And handsome. They seem a bit young, though." She scrunched her nose, giving him a pity-you look. If she hadn't pouted her lips, he would have taken her seriously. "That must be exhausting, an old man like you trying to keep them satisfied. You poor bastard."

"Old man?" He grinned, then rubbed a hand over his chest. "Yes, keeping them satisfied is arduous work and time-consuming."

The waiter served their drinks. Cam opened her water, pouring half a glass for her. She let him and had expected him to do so. He liked that. He'd dated women who thought he disrespected them by pouring their drinks. Tessa didn't care either way.

"That woman in the corner seems nice," she said with a nudge of her head. Her hair cascaded over one shoulder, looking soft and releasing the fruity fragrance of her shampoo. "Don't look now. Wow, we need to work on your skills."

Cam laughed and turned in slow, exaggerated movements, drawing a chuckle from her. He looked past the models and party girls to the woman alone at a table. Late thirties, dark lustrous hair curling down her back. She wore jeans and a simple pink shirt. A jacket lay on the chair beside her.

"She looks sad," he said. "Don't look now." He fake-gasped then shook his head. "We've got to work on your skills."

Tessa laughed, throwing her head back to do so. The sound was throaty, full-bodied. He loved hearing it. "Okay, so maybe sad is a no-go. I'd take your age, the usual tart's, and aim for the middle. That's the range you should look at. Younger than you but not too immature. She should have wealth or a career, so yours wouldn't matter."

"Shopping for a date for me?" He didn't know how he felt about that. After all, he'd said this was a thank-you dinner, therefore, not romantic.

His pizza arrived, and he leaned back for the waiter to place it on the table. She fell silent, sipping her water, wrapping those red lips around the edge of the glass.

"Not hungry at all?" He raised a slice to his mouth.

"No, and definitely not for pizza. Don't mind me. There's bound to be a woman here suitable for your refined tastes." She gestured to his Guinness. He smiled around his full mouth. "I'm a little nervous for tomorrow. I'm meeting a publisher. It's hard for an unknown writer, especially from Africa, to make it in the literary world without an agent. I opted to self-publish rather than wait."

"You'll do fine. What started you down this path?" He ate and studied her as she glossed over her history, gesturing with her hands, her joy and laughter frequent. She loved to write.

"After the meeting, I'll return to the hotel and check out." A sadness flitted across her face, and she forced it away with another smile. "My trip's almost done. A few friends to visit then home." Her breath hitched, and she raised the glass to her lips with trembling hands. Her chocolate eyes shimmered, and she remained silent as if she couldn't trust her voice.

"Can you have dessert?" He chose to change the subject rather than discuss what she was feeling.

She chuckled, gave him a grateful look, and shook her head. "I wish. As you get older, your body decides what you can or cannot eat. For some people, they must live on tofu. For me, it's non-dairy."

"And I bring you to a pizza place." He frowned. "Even offered you a slice."

"I was tempted, but I'd pay for it. Sometimes it's worth it, though."

He swirled the dregs of his stout before taking a sip. "It feels weird, me eating, drinking, and you with your water."

"If it was lunchtime, I'd smash my face with bacon, eggs, and delicious coffee. I'd look like a ravenous beast." She beamed and clinked her water glass against his pint glass.

"What time's your meeting tomorrow?"

"Eleven, which means I'll be starving the entire time." She shrugged, her fingers toying with the napkin again.

"We'll do lunch afterward." Just like that, he would see her again.

Her gaze shot up to meet his, her surprise clear. "But this was a thank-you dinner. You don't have to take me to lunch, as well."

"I think we can squeeze in one more." He bit into his pizza and nodded, letting her know his mind was firm on this.

"Then I'll pay," she said.

He blinked, unsure he'd heard her correctly. "Are you offering to buy a wealthy man lunch?"

She laughed, shaking her head from side-to-side. "You're acting like that's a rare thing. No, I'm not paying, my company is, well, sort of. They give me an allowance, and usually, I buy my children gifts, but they're adults now, so this time, it's all for me."

"All right, you can pay; on one condition." A smirk crept into place.

Chapter Four

"Let me hear it." Tessa arched a brow and narrowed her eyes in suspicion.

"The rest of the day is on me."

"Since it's just lunch, then hell yeah, I'll agree to that." She looked so pleased with herself, he found himself chuckling.

He paid the bill and escorted her out, ignoring the women casting glances at him. Tessa was right; they were young. He shifted his hand higher until it splayed across her shoulders; her warmth seeping through to tantalize him. Her hair caressed his skin with each step she took.

"Shall we stroll along the pavement for a while?" He didn't want to climb into his car and return her to the hotel.

She slipped her arm through the crook of his and rested her forehead on his shoulder. No makeup smeared off, and with a start, he realized she didn't wear any.

"Would you eat dinner if it was at a restaurant in Paris?"

"Yes, as long as it wasn't frog's legs." She scrunched up her nose; it was adorable.

"Want to fly across tonight?" He envisioned seeing her expressions, her joy as she took in the Parisian delights.

"What? Why?" She peered at him with her brow furrowing.

"Because I'm rich, and we can." He shrugged, trying to hide how much he'd love for her to say yes. The desire to spoil her should've concerned him. He distrusted women, including his sister.

"If you had plans to do so and there was a spare seat, then yes. But no if it's just for me." She shook her head, sending her hair flying. They caught the setting sunlight and glittered copper.

"Why not?" He almost demanded she let him spoil her. Oh, how things had turned. At first, he'd thought her a spy out to milk him for money or information, but when he threw his wealth at her, she wasn't interested.

"You've known me less than a day. I wouldn't ask a friend of ten years. It's an abuse of friendship, that's what it is." She huffed.

He liked that too but released a long sigh of disappointment even though he admired her conviction. "What about a diamond bracelet?"

"Are you testing me, Cam?" She arched a brow. "Am I wearing any jewelry now?" He glanced at her ears, her neck, and her hands devoid of adornment. "Not much into that."

"So, what would a friend give you as a gift?"

"I received notebooks once with a beautiful pen. I cried." She flicked a glare at him. "I don't cry unless I'm angry, frustrated, or something bad has happened. When I opened the wrapping and saw the gift, it was as if she understood me, what made me happy. I love gadgets too, Kindles, MP3 players, tablets but will only buy if I need them."

"You'd be hard to shop for," he said.

"Gifts don't mean the same as when I was young. Now, if I need or want it, I can afford to buy it."

"Let me see, a woman not too old, nor too young, of independent means and sexy. It sounds as if you want me to date you." He couldn't resist teasing her.

She laughed. "I did describe me, didn't I? It's a good thing I'm married then, or else I'd be after your gorgeous ass."

"Would you?" Everything within him stilled as he held his breath.

"No." She gave him a sheepish smile. "I've never noticed when a guy liked me. I wouldn't know how to cougar if you paid me too."

"If a guy told you he liked you?"

"First, I'd have to get over the shock of it," she said.

He scowled. "I didn't think you'd have low self-esteem." He hooked her around the waist to tug her closer, allowing a jogger to whisk past them. He didn't release her, enjoying her tantalizing scent and the softness of her curves pressed against him. She trembled in his arms.

"All women do, but that's not the reason for the shock. I'm oblivious, going through life in my world and just being me." She shrugged, peering at him before pushing away.

He let her with a little reluctance. "Did you have plans for tonight?" She might have to entertain colleagues or any of those men who had admired her this afternoon.

"After last night's debacle, I planned to curl up in bed, maybe write a chapter or two while watching your telly."

"We can still do that." He envisioned sprawling with her head resting on his shoulder, flicking through the channels. The image whispered of contentment, something he hadn't felt in years, if ever.

"We?" Her brow furrowed, confirming her words. She didn't have a clue he liked her.

"You don't think I'm saying goodbye anytime soon, do you?" He tightened his arm around her waist, hoping to convey he had no intention of releasing her.

"Of course I am. Thank-you dinner and cheerio." She waved her hand, startling a passing pedestrian who waved back.

"That's cold, Tess," he said. "Using me for a bottle of sparkling water and setting me free. I'm deeply hurt."

"Nonsense." She laughed. "The truth is, you walking into the hotel or my room is noticeable. People will think the worst, and I have a professional reputation to maintain."

"Ah, a valid reason. Okay, not the hotel, how about my home?" He glanced away, searching for the car to hide his eagerness. He could see her in his kitchen and his bed. The imagery fluttered his heartbeat. His cock pulsed in anticipation.

"No, I don't know you well enough. Despite the time we spent together, I could turn out to be a white-rabbit killer, then where would you be?"

"Putting you on a plane to Africa?" He chuckled and ushered her toward the car Anthony had double-parked.

"Good point." She smirked, looking impressed at his comeback.

"Then the club? You might get to dance this time."

"Oh, that's low." She climbed into the car. "All right, but not too late. You need your beauty sleep."

"Me?" He slid in alongside her, making sure his thigh pressed along the length of hers.

"Of the two of us, you're the pretty one. For me, sleep provides my next chapter or novel." Her smile ended on a breathless sigh.

She admired the passing scenery with the Shard in the distance and splayed her hand on the window. She had long fingers, square palms on small hands. Her nails were nude and short, no blood-red talons to scrape his back. It was a pity; just the thought had him hardening farther. He gathered her other hand in his to study it, tapping each fingertip.

"Why the short bare nails?"

"Almost ripped off a nail when sensei stripped me of a rubber gun. Since then, it seemed wiser to keep them short. No nail coloring because I'm far from home, and carting polish remover across continents was a waste of luggage space."

"So practical," he teased, laced his fingers through hers, and rested their clasped hands on his knee.

Her touch burned him, sending shivers of excitement outward and up toward his throbbing arousal. He shifted, hoping to ease the ache and loosen his jeans a little. His hand dwarfed hers. A white strip showed where her wedding ring had once been. He stroked his thumb over it, and she sucked in a sharp breath.

He lifted his gaze to meet hers. "I'm sorry," he said, referring to her suffering, but he wasn't apologizing for her being, in a way, single.

"I should've seen it coming. He worked later and later, and I spent all my time honing my writing craft. The most horrifying realization is that I'm on my own again." She shrugged, but it looked forced, with pain and fear darkening her chocolate eyes.

"I'm glad to have met you."

She stared at him for a long moment. "Marc's tart?" she teased, squeezing his hand.

"I did apologize." He gave her a pointed look.

"Yes, you did, but it's still funny." Her red lips curled, enchanting him.

He leaned forward to taste her, but the car drew to a halt outside the club. It was early with the arrival of night staff still hours away. There would be no music playing, and they'd be alone in his office. Damn, when had he last entertained a woman there? One he wanted as much as he did Tessa?

He bounded out of the car and offered her his hand. She placed hers in his without hesitation, her trust precious. Last night when she'd doubted Doc's skill, Cam had cupped her face and lost himself in her big brown eyes. Her trust had been breathtaking then, too. Looping her arm through his, he trapped her hand on his forearm and escorted her inside. The cleaning staff scurried around, the sting of bleach driving him up the stairs to his office.

"Hi, Tessa," Marc said from behind the desk. He spent the afternoon doing the previous evening's finances. Pushing the chair back, he rose as if Cam wanted to work. "It's good to see you. How's your thigh?"

"Hey, Marc." She waved. "A little stiff, but the painkillers helped, so thanks for that." She hid her mouth behind her hand and stage-whispered, "I might need a rescue later. Cam doesn't want to drop me off at the hotel."

"It will cost you," Marc teased.

Cam growled, not liking the implication of his words. She frowned at him, her smile faltering, but it returned when her gaze settled on Marc again.

"Okay, let's hear it," she said. "What will it be?"

"A dance." Marc narrowed his eyes at Cam.

"Sure, as long as it's not the Tango. I struggle to move between a man's thighs." She drew away from Cam to approach the glass wall, unaware of the sensuality of her words. He adjusted his jeans around his erection and shot Marc a warning look. There would be no dancing.

"Speaking of thighs, I do believe yours is bleeding," Marc said.

She gasped and twisted to look at the back of her skirt.

"Oh, no, this is my favorite skirt." Her distress lowered her voice, making it huskier. With her sexy accent, it devastated Cam's senses, sending tingles along his neck and shoulders.

"Cam can try to remove the stain." Marc gestured to him, offering his untried cleaning services.

She pinched her lips and shook her head, tossing her hair wild.

"It's fine. It's just a skirt." She tried to dismiss their offer and the ruined skirt, but her lips pouted. Whatever she was feeling was on her face, and Cam liked that about her.

"Wear one of our T-shirts. Should be longer than last night's dress. If I can't clean the blood, then it will dry, and you can wear the skirt again." He removed a shirt out of the cupboard and offered it to her. "Besides, we'll need to have Doc look at it. You might have pulled a stitch."

"This London trip gets better and better. I should cut my losses and run." She accepted the shirt from him and nudged her head at the door. "I need to change; out you two go."

Opening a cupboard door, he revealed the secret entrance to an en suite. "Use the bathroom." He chuckled at her wide eyes as she strode in and closed the door behind her.

"How did it go?" Marc kept his voice low.

"Out." Cam pointed at the office door.

His friend leaving with laughter trailing him stiffened Cam's shoulders. He'd made no progress; hell, she didn't even realize he was into her. He rushed to his desk and slid onto the chair, tapping on the keyboard as he did so. The security feeds switched to the bathroom.

He couldn't see her, and with a start, he realized she'd popped her head out the door.

"Cam, would you mind if I showered? I'd like to be clean when Doc comes, then I won't need to call the nurse tomorrow morning."

"Sure." He cleared his throat, ignoring the guilt dominating his mind. "Use whatever you need."

Disappearing with a hurried "thanks," she reappeared on the security feed.

She unbuckled her belt, draping it over the closed toilet seat. Then tugged the shirt free of the skirt's waistband, unbuttoned it, and slipped it off. A white bustier hugged her torso, changing the sexy outfit to something out of a lingerie catalog. She unclipped the bustier and freed her breasts. They had a natural bounce to them when she took the time to massage them. She had large nipples with wide areolas, a dark musk against her pale skin.

She unzipped the skirt and shimmied out of it, raising it to study the stain. It hid her body from view but not her reaction to the damage. Sadness slouched her shoulders. She folded the skirt and placed it on the vanity.

The full sight of her punched through him, lust consuming his restraint and pumping his heart rate. He shoved the guilt aside and focused on the indent of her waist he'd touched many times today. The curve of her hip and the tattoo at the base of her spine. That wasn't what had him trembling with need, his cock harder than marble.

It was the realization she hadn't worn panties. Now he understood her reticence and subsequent blush.

Fuck.

Chapter Five

Tessa stepped under the shower spray with music playing from her phone. She plunged her head in as she swayed to the rhythm, taking the time to wash her face and hair. Because it would be rude, she didn't want to take too long. Raising her arms, she rinsed her hair one more time, checked the blood had washed off her thigh, then switched off the water. Wringing out her hair, she stepped onto the floor mat before snatching a towel off the rack.

After wrapping it around her head, she took another to dry her body. The songs changed, and she altered her movements, singing along, but the entire time, doubts plagued her. She should leave, bid Cam farewell, but something in his eyes kept her with him. He could make her heart flutter with one look. She hated yet loved being here. It was a new experience for her. Now she'd be in a shirt, sans panties, while Doc looked at her thigh. A vulnerable situation, but she couldn't tell Cam why she didn't want him to save her skirt. He'd think she was hitting on him.

Her stomach wrenched, and she peered at herself in the mirror. Her flushed face and smeared mascara had her sighing. Right. Like he'd believe that. She pursed her lips at her reflection. After neatening her eyeliner with a fingertip, she dropped the towel and donned what garments she could. Bustier, check. The T-shirt, check. It reached past her knees, but still, the cool air kissing her butt cheeks reminded her of her vulnerability.

Opening the door, she stepped through it, crossing the office to hand Cam her skirt. He was behind his desk, typing on his computer but had compressed his lips as if he were in pain. She hesitated, not wanting to intrude. He'd offered, but it seemed a tad intimate.

He snatched the skirt from her before she could retreat and gestured to the small bar fridge under the basin.

"Help yourself." He unfolded her skirt and ironed it out on his desk with the flat of his hand. Alongside him, sat a cup of vinegar, and he dipped a finger in to rub across the stain. She peered over his shoulder to watch the blood fade. "I'd like a soda if you're getting." He looked at her.

She stilled.

Their faces were inches apart. She jerked back, having leaned into him. A little lower and she would've tasted those lush lips of his.

"Sure, which one?" She bolted for the fridge, relishing the inside chill cooling her cheeks.

One diet soda was tucked at the back. She snatched it for herself and twisted to look at Cam, waiting for his choice. He stared at the back of her legs, and she straightened, having forgotten she was barely covered.

"You choose." His voice grated across her nerves and sent butterflies skydiving through her insides.

She dropped to her haunches, wincing when the stitches pulled tight, and chose a popular brand. After peeling the tab, she placed the can in front of him. He sprinkled white powder over the stain and scooped up the can to hold it to his lips.

"Bicarb," he said.

She nodded. It sterilized when added to vinegar, but would it suck the blood out of fabric, as sand did to oil?

Sitting on the edge of the couch, she watched him while sipping her soda. He held out a remote and pressed it. On one wall, panels slid open, and a massive television screen appeared, coming to life on a sports channel. He typed something on his keyboard and strode around his desk, holding the remote to her.

"I'm taking a quick shower. Here, watch some telly."

She grabbed it with a smile and placed the soda on the coffee table to recline on the couch. Leaning her back against the armrest, she bent her legs to elevate her thighs off the leather and flicked through the channels. The door clicking shut behind her had her releasing a pent-up breath. There was a new tension in the room she didn't understand. For the first time since meeting Cam, her instincts reacted like she was in dangerous territory.

She should leave, should run from whatever was happening here. Guys liked to hang out with her since she was surprisingly devoid of female drama. She assumed Cam felt the same, and having this handsome man's attention was like rain on arid land. Her heart ached for it, to be noticed, or appreciated. She'd wait for Doc because medical fees were expensive, then she'd bid them goodbye.

The thought of never hearing Cam's raspy voice was a sad one. She liked him, his charm, his smile, and the darker thoughts that furrowed his brow. He was a complex man, showing his best side to her; kind and chivalric, but most men wanted something. She just hadn't figured out what was behind his intense gaze.

"Where's Mathews?" A woman stepped into the office, trailed by a friend.

Tessa stiffened. Fury flowed off the stranger, the air thickening with malevolence. Cam's girlfriend? No. The way her friend shifted from foot to foot with her gaze darting, said this wasn't a romantic visit. Climbing off the couch with care, Tessa dropped the remote on the coffee table, then faced them.

"Who wants to know?" she asked and almost chuckled. What was this? A movie scene?

"Listen, you tart, I've come for him, for what his men did to my brother. Where. Is. Mathews?"

The tiny, tattooed bundle of rage didn't intimidate Tessa. There were men in Krav Maga class who had arms the size of tree trunks. Whenever they charged her, adrenaline would fire all her circuits. This woman wouldn't be a problem to handle.

Tart? She laughed. In future, reading apple tart on a dessert menu might trigger memories of this trip. "I wouldn't know. I'm Marc's tart. What happened to your brother?"

"He was beaten last night and is in A&E with a broken jaw." The woman's face twinged with sibling concern. Broken jaw? Bart's fist could do that.

Tessa stilled. "Did he come with two friends wielding knives?"

"Yes."

"I was there." Silence met her announcement.

The woman stiffened, her face contorting with fury. "You're the bitch..." She stepped closer, her posture menacing.

Tessa strolled around the couch with the glass wall at her back. If there was a fight, she needed space to move. Dammit, her thigh was never going to heal.

"Yes, and he drew a knife on the bouncer. If I was you, I'd get the facts straight." She placed the blame on her brother's idiotic shoulders.

"Their target was the bouncer, bitch." The woman tugged a knife from her belt and lunged.

Tessa snorted. Stupidity must run in the family.

Chapter Six

Cam shuddered as he peeled off his jeans. His hard cock sprang free, and he gave it a rough rub, closing his eyes at the exquisite torture his touch inflicted. He shouldn't have watched her shower, but moments in privacy revealed the truth about a person. Hers had shown what she was.

A woman on the cusp of divorce and sexier than she had a right to be. The way she had shampooed her hair and gyrated her hips as if she listened to music... He recalled with clarity her breasts lifting every time she raised her arms. Scars marred her lower abdomen, and he had no right to judge her for it. His body was as weathered, having survived knife and bullet wounds. Hers were from giving life, his were from when he'd taken lives or the consequences thereof.

He stepped into the cubicle and sucked in a breath when icy water rushed to cool his ardor. For a moment, he was tempted to take care of his arousal, which bobbed in eagerness. He ignored it and washed his hair while shooting glances at the monitors he'd summoned from their hidden alcoves. He could watch his office and club when he was at his most vulnerable. Tessa hadn't moved from the couch, and in the black-and-white image, the smoothness of her legs glowed pale.

Turning up the heat, he rinsed his hair, raising his face to the spray. He'd have to tell her soon. Maybe he should kiss her and find out that way? He liked that idea better. Wiping water off his face, he watched her spin toward the door and speak to someone. Her movements were jerky, like a tiger attuned to danger. She climbed off the couch and looped around it, her posture coiled. *Fuck.*

He switched off the water and stepped out of the shower to run a towel over his legs with his focus fixed on the screens. The images blurred as she punched and kicked, sending a woman flying.

Who the fuck is that?

He yanked his jeans on, not bothering to button them, and bolted out the bathroom. At the base of one wall, a woman lay slumped. Another woman received a punch to her face. She cried out and charged, her fingers in claws as blood dribbled down her chin. Tessa dodged her attacks with ease then uppercut the woman, sending her stumbling.

"What the fuck is going on?" he asked, his voice booming. Who'd dare enter his office and threaten his...what? Woman? Lover? Friend? His...Tessa.

"Oh, good. You're just in time. You have a visitor." Tessa swept damp hair out of her face. It had darkened and curled around her in wild disarray.

His lips twitched, and despite the situation, the warmth of humor filled his chest. He took a step toward her, needing to kiss her right now.

"Mathews?" The bleeding woman coughed, spitting onto his wooden floor.

"Yes, who wants to know?" He folded his arms across his chest, ignoring a snigger from Tessa. That she found this funny as he did softened the red circling his vision.

"One of your men sent my brother to A&E with a busted jaw. The police are outside his room, waiting to arrest him. I demand you dismiss the charges. One more infraction, then he's back in prison."

"I didn't force him to bring a knife to my club. You should be yelling at your brother." Cam pressed a button mounted on the wall. "Yet, you had the audacity to come into my office and attack my guest. How stupid are you?" His voice was soft, but he vibrated with fury; his fingers clenched and unfurled. Had she thought to bring a gun, who knew how much danger Tessa would've been in. "I'll bring this to Logan's attention, and whether your brother survives prison is for him to decide."

Stumbling back, she paled and shook her head, fear twisting her features. Marc burst in with another bouncer, Allan, trailing him. He must have just arrived for the first shift since he was still in his casual clothes.

"What? Who is...? How the hell did they get in here?" Marc gestured to both women.

Cam rolled his tense shoulders, hoping to ease the burn between them. "I don't know. Deliver them to the police. Charge them with trespassing and assault."

"Assault?" Marc ran his eyes over Cam then spun on Tessa. "Not again, Tess-luv."

She shrugged as if caught brawling was the norm for her. "I was just watching your telly." She raised her palms.

Marc chuckled, gripped the bleeding woman by the arm, and escorted her out. Allan followed with the unconscious woman over his shoulder. He closed the office door behind him.

Cam faced Tessa, then crossed the room with swift strides. He drew her into his arms, and she let him, cuddling into his embrace.

"Are you all right?" He buried his face in her cool, damp hair.

"I'm fine. I'm starting to think Londoners are bat-shit crazy, or your club is cursed."

"Maybe both?" He slid his hands along her arms to cup her elbows. Water trickled down his torso from his wet hair. It didn't matter, despite the goosebumps forming.

"Now that the drama is behind us, how about drying your hair and putting on a shirt?" She raised her gaze to meet his. Her eyes warmed with admiration. Now, that was a good sign he wasn't alone in the aroused department.

He grinned. "What? Why?" he asked, choosing to tease her. "I'm topless, you're bottomless."

She grinned, glanced down to hide her pinkening cheeks, then shuffled back, forcing him to drop his hands. He didn't want to. He wanted to follow her until he had her pinned against the glass and at his mercy.

"When's Doc arriving?" She plucked an imaginary lint off the T-shirt.

"Most staff arrive after eight. Why? Are you in pain?" He scanned her, looking for new injuries. "You said you were fine." His tone was accusatory when he gripped her by the shoulders and spun her. The sight of blood streaming down her thigh drew a gasp from him. "Bloody hell, Tessa, why didn't you say something?"

"I'm still fine, just bleeding. For the sake of peace, I busted up my knuckles too." She showed him her right hand, bruised and lacerated.

"On the couch, now." He clenched his jaw, disbelieving she was hurt again. Her disregard for it made him so furious, he wanted to wrap her in cotton wool or his arms and protect her from further harm.

"It makes more sense to wash off the blood in the bathroom. A quick hop in the shower, and it's done."

He grumbled, not liking her logic but agreeing she was right. At his nod, she hurried past him. "I'll have ice ready and Doc on the way."

He didn't watch her on the screens, not this time. While drying himself, he ordered the ice and checked when Doc would arrive. As he took a shirt out of the cupboard, the bathroom door opened.

"I bled all over the T-shirt," she said with a scowl. "All those monitors? More security? Did you learn the lesson the hard way, or are you paranoid?"

She trailed a fingertip along the scar streaking his left side. He shivered, grabbed her hand in his, and trapped it against his abdomen. Her touch burned him and set his senses ablaze.

"Hard lesson," he said, his voice harsh as he spoke over the lump in his throat. He liked her touch, liked her standing before him, loved the enticement of her, and her relaxed temperament.

"On the couch now, boss?" Her still-ruby lips curled upward. "Will I sprawl there until Doc arrives?"

"Maybe not, but I need to take a look. If the bleeding hasn't stopped, I reserve the right to panic."

"You? Panic?" She laughed, climbing onto the couch to spread out on it. This time she was less respectful of his leather, but she was barefoot, so her caution wasn't necessary. She took the time to make sure the shirt covered her backside, but now he knew why. As she'd done yesterday, she rested her chin on her overlapping hands on the armrest.

He slipped the T-shirt on before kneeling beside her. "Are you hungry?"

He needed a safe topic, one that drew his attention from her smooth thigh curving upward into a bare ass. His hand trembled when he pinched her shirt's hem between forefinger and thumb to lift it an inch since it covered her wound. He was careful not to expose too much of her to his greedy gaze. She didn't stiffen, didn't glance back; trusting him to care for her. That trust was the only thing keeping him honorable.

"No, but after this episode, I'm tempted to have a shot of alcohol." She dropped her forehead onto her hands with a sigh.

He studied her wound with a frown. She'd pulled out a few stitches, and blood still oozed but not alarmingly. Rising, he fetched the first aid box and returned to dab on antiseptic with a cotton swab as he'd done yesterday. This time, he planned to caress her skin again, liking that she shivered every time he touched her.

"How bad is it?" she asked minutes later. "Your silence has me worried."

"Worst case scenario," he said. "Please sit up. Let me bandage you."

She nodded, and with careful movements, perched her backside on the edge of the seat.

He nudged her thighs apart, drawing her gasp. She didn't say anything, preferring to nibble on her bottom lip as he longed to do.

"Cam?" She watched him as he wrapped the bandage around her thigh. He pinned it with the clasp and grabbed the ice bucket, holding it for her to plunge her hand in. "What's the real reason for the dinner invitation?" She raised her chin, a sign of her stubborn nature and courage.

He chose honesty. "I can't get you out of my mind."

She sucked in a startled breath and blinked at him, studying his face in the artificial light. "Like I'm a puzzle you need to unravel?"

"If by unravel, you mean strip every item of clothing off your body, then yes." He waited for her reaction.

She trembled; her breathing became erratic. "You don't know any tarts?" She blessed him with a teasing smile, falling on humor to hide her shyness.

"I do, but not many ladies." He moved the ice bowl away, placing it on the coffee table behind him. She dried her hand on her shirt like they weren't discussing something important.

"Nice response." She laughed. "Smooth."

The flash of her white teeth against her red lips had him leaning closer. He inhaled the scent of her skin under his soap, shifting nearer to run his nose along the arch of her throat.

"You smell amazing." He cleared his throat. "I don't like your lipstick."

"Too red?" she asked, her voice husky. Marc was right. Her sexy accent was an aphrodisiac on its own, licking at his crumbling control.

"I want to nibble it off you." And did he. Bloody hell, she was killing him without trying.

She laughed again. "You can try. It's long-lasting." When she scraped her bottom lip along her teeth, it made no impact on the lipstick. "See."

That explained why it hadn't faded since the hotel. He grasped her knees and spread her thighs on another of her gasps. Ignoring it, he shuffled into the 'V' of her legs to glide his hands from her hips to her spine and up.

"What are you doing?" Her beguiling eyes grew wider, her voice sultry.

"You said I could try." He brushed his lips across her parted ones, savoring her breath mingling with his. Faced with his craving, he slowed, choosing to extend the moment. "Tessa," he groaned, brushing his lips back and forth before gliding the tip of his tongue into the warm, silken depths of her mouth.

Her fingers dug into his biceps—one hand icy-cold—before sliding up to grip his hair. When she met his forage with her own, his resistance evaporated, and he crushed her to him, smashing his mouth across hers. With tiny flicks of her tongue, she scattered his thoughts and snatched his ability to breathe. His nipples hardened, and he shuddered, desire throbbing along the length of his cock.

The waiting was worth it; to have her in his arms, at last.

"Marc said I should come straight up. Want me to return later?" Doc asked from the door.

Cam grumbled, not appreciating the intrusion but valuing Doc's early arrival because she did need him.

"No." Cam brushed her hair behind her ears. She looked dazed; her eyes were heavy-lidded, the desire intense. "Fuck," he whispered, dipping his head to snatch a hard kiss. He shifted back on his knees, bemoaning the loss of her heat. "Tessa has pulled stitches, and her knuckles need attention. I wrapped her thigh, not knowing how long you'd be."

"Wish you hadn't come to Elysium?" Doc stepped into the room with his medkit in hand.

"I'm torn." Her voice rasped along Cam's senses.

Preferring to face the glass window than watch her sprawl on the couch again, he stepped aside. He was just a man and a weak one at that. Without a second thought, he'd have taken her here, now. But she was in pain, injured. How desperate was he?

He snuck a glance in time to see Doc flash the curve of her ass. Cam gave a decisive nod, blaming her for his condition, before dragging his focus to the empty dance floor below. It was an hour before opening time, and his staff scurried around attending to their tasks.

"I'm serious this time." Doc's words drew Cam back to the moment. How long had he stood there, lost in thought? "Take it easy, please, Tessa."

"I'll try." Her voice was soft but filled with determination. Doc closed his bag, gestured to the pain meds on the counter, and left. "That was sweet of him to come in earlier."

She twisted off the couch and reached for the bottle despite Doc's instructions to take care. Cam grabbed it before she could and uncapped it, shaking two onto her palm. Grabbing her soda, he offered it to her, and she smiled her thanks.

Flipping the back of the couch down, he fetched two pillows out of the cupboard, lay down on the leather, and with the remote in hand, gestured to her to curl up beside him. She watched him, her mouth gaping. But when he arched a brow, she sprawled beside him, rested her cheek on his shoulder and her bruised hand on his chest.

"What do you want to watch?" He kissed her temple and tightened his arm around her.

"I don't care." She snuggled closer and buried her face in his T-shirt to smother a yawn. "Pain meds make me sleepy, so if I drift off, wake me before six. I'm meeting Owen for breakfast."

"Breakfast?" The jealousy burning through him was unnecessary. Owen's wedding ring and brotherly affection toward her meant Cam had nothing to worry about, yet he didn't like her spending time with him.

"He eats, I watch," she said. "Tomorrow's his last day here, and he has my laptop. I also need to pack and check out." She fell silent, her nose still pressed against his chest. "You smell good too," she mumbled minutes later. "Thank you for the kiss. I'll always cherish it."

Her whispered words tore through him, more devastating than if she'd yelled them. He couldn't breathe with something squeezing his chest. No one had thanked him for a kiss before, and she'd done so without ulterior motives. Fuck, the woman had such a hold on him, pitting his heart against his cock.

There were seven more days before her return flight, and he had every intention of kissing her again.

Chapter Seven

Tessa awoke with a start. Darkness engulfed her, and she struggled to find her bearings. Lying alongside a man was her first realization. She'd curled against Cam, his arms wrapped around her since he lay on his side. It was a strange experience for her. Forest wasn't an affectionate man and had left her to sleep on her side of the bed.

Cam had kissed her, and what a kiss. Her toes tingled in memory of his lips claiming hers. She'd been helpless to fight him and had to admit, she hadn't wanted to. He was a virile man with his charisma off the charts, and despite this, she sensed a core of steel. Yet he chose to spend time with her. What did he want from her? What did he stand to gain? A romp and goodbye? The way those women had fawned over him, he didn't lack in the romp department.

Pain pulsed in her thigh and hand, matching her heartbeat since the painkillers had worn off. She considered stumbling in the dark to look for the pills, but the thought of disturbing his sleep and saying goodbye to the comfort of his arms was worse than the pain. So, she snuggled deeper into his embrace, nuzzling his T-shirt-sculpted chest with her nose, and tightening her arm around his waist.

She relived the moment when he'd burst out of the bathroom in nothing but an unbuttoned pair of jeans. Holy cow, he'd stolen her breath, her focus, just by standing there. No man had a right to be that devastating. His chest and torso sported entwining tattoos—angel's wings curved around his shoulder blades. Words written in Latin dipped over one side. They were beautiful, electrifying, sending sparks of need to coil within her.

"What's wrong?" Sleep thickened his voice with an added layer of sex appeal he didn't need. "Are you in pain?"

"I am, but I don't want to move."

He shifted, withdrawing his arms, but she squeezed, clinging to him.

"I don't want you to move either."

"Tess, sweetheart, I'll come right back," he said.

"Nope, the moment will be lost. Please." She pinched her mouth shut, realizing she was pleading with him. This was it for her. Once he stood up, he'd have Anthony take her home. Who knew when next she'd cuddle a man? He encircled her with his arms, and she released her held breath.

"Better?" There was humor in his voice.

"Yes." She inhaled the spicy scent of him.

"You're being silly." He buried his face in her neck, placing a kiss there that sent shivers rocketing through her.

He trailed his open mouth up to nibble on her earlobe. Her core pulsed in response, and she dug her fingers into the taut muscle of his back.

"You know this makes no sense, Cam." Not to her. It was strange to kiss a man other than Forest. That wouldn't stop her, though. How many lovers had her husband had that she didn't know of? The thought had her fighting a wave of nausea. She'd undergone tests to ensure she was clean, but it didn't ease the filthiness layering her soul.

"What makes no sense?" Cam didn't cease pressing his soft lips to her skin.

She shivered, her nipples pebbling within her loose bustier. Had he unclipped her? She moaned at the realization he knew she went commando. Dammit. What must he think of her?

"You kissing me."

He stilled and clapped his hands, startling her as did the blinding lights. One look at the aroused intensity in his blue eyes had the breath rushing out of her. Hot damn, he did desire her. The insanity of it curled a smile across her face, zinging joy through her heart.

"I had you investigated because I couldn't believe your sweetness wasn't a disguise. But I wanted you from the moment you sassed me."

"I was cheeky to you?" That did sound like her, but what she said or did, she couldn't recall.

"Something about a rat's ass." He flipped her onto her back then spread her knees with his hips, raising her bandaged leg to rest against his chest. He glided his hand from her knee, down her thigh to her bare hip, taking the T-shirt with it. "Feel how much I want you, Tess."

When he swooped in for a heart-wrenching kiss, he rubbed something hard against her. He trailed his fingers up her stomach then stilled when he encountered the bustier. He splayed out his hands, circling her ribs to lift her and rip the T-shirt off her.

She gasped and clung to his chest, trying to hide her body from him. He clicked his tongue, pushed her against the armrest, and sipped from her lips, his breathing ragged.

"Never hide what you sacrificed for love," he said with his touch feathering across her shoulders, hooking the straps with his fingers, and gliding them off her.

"Cam." She splayed her hands on his chest, halting his seduction. "We need to talk."

"No, we don't." He grasped her upper arms.

"Yes, we do." She met his gaze, snatched a kiss, then smiled, trying to convey she wasn't rejecting him. "We need protection and a towel."

He released his breath and blessed her with a sensual grin, dimpling a cheek, as well. "Protection is a given, but I don't care about the bloody leather, Tess."

"Um, it's not for the leather." She glanced down, chewing on her bottom lip as heat stained her cheeks. How to tell him something so personal? "My orgasms are...messy." There, she'd said it.

"In what way?" His stroking fingers stilled with something potent darkening his face.

"You're honestly going to make me spell it out?" She shifted as much as the position allowed without impaling herself on his solid length.

"No," he said, his voice hoarse. Grabbing the discarded shirt, he spread it under her backside, then took a condom from his back pocket. He waved it at her before placing it on the couch beside them. "Happy?"

Not waiting for her answer, he sealed his lips to hers, his hands clasping her face, holding her still for his onslaught. She succumbed, unable to fight this much passion. And she struggled with the gratitude that had her clinging to him. Seconds later, cool air kissed her breasts when he removed her bustier. His hands warmed her skin, his touch gentle. She moaned, arching into him, then looped her right leg around him, tugging him closer.

"Wait," he said.

She let her leg slip off him as he bounded off the couch.

He tore off his T-shirt and tossed it aside, before sliding off his still-undone jeans. It had to be the most incredible visual delight she'd experienced. He didn't allow her the time to admire him, returning to lift her wounded thigh onto his chest. Before she could say something, he leaned his pelvis forward, and his hard erection teased her. He twisted to press his palm lower, and she raised her hips to encourage him. His touch stilled, and he shuddered, growling her name.

"You shave?" The words were barely discernible in his gruff voice. She nodded, to which he groaned, "You're killing me, robbing me of honor. I wanted to pleasure you first."

The thought of another hour of foreplay, as delicious as the idea was, had her shaking her head. She needed him in her. Now.

"Go ahead, Cam. I won't judge," she said with a wink. "I have one condition, though."

"What?" he asked.

"I want fast and deep thrusts."

At her words, he raised his eyes to the ceiling, sucking in calming breaths before tearing open the wrapper with his teeth and working the condom on. She hadn't taken the time to look at him, to see how much he wanted her. Perhaps she would've another opportunity, but if this was it for her, then she'd find contentment in that.

Within seconds, he repositioned himself at her entrance, dipped the head of his cock in before gliding in. He grunted, his fingers embedding in her hips as if to hold her still. The length of him stretching her had her moaning, her body arching as he filled her. The novelty of him had her panting. Once buried deep within her, he gave her a toe-curling kiss. His lips demanded a response from her, claimed her breath, and set her heart dancing.

"You feel incredible." He withdrew and thrust into her.

She whimpered. Lights danced in her vision as exquisite pleasure skittered along her spine. She writhed, pausing every few minutes for a teasing orgasm, until with one hard thrust, she cried out, a potent joy flooding her, focusing her mind, her world on the man pounding into her.

As his rhythm increased, he took her over the edge again, pleasure after pleasure coursing through her. He roared, his pelvis stilling as he arched his back. He gripped her hips again, and his white teeth dimpling his bottom lip. An intensity crossed his features like he was in pain. He sucked in great breaths, and a light sheen of sweat coated his chest. Leveling his blue gaze on her, a sensual smile curled his upper lip, and he kissed her again.

"I've never felt that before," he said, between kisses. "When you orgasm, it flushes heat along the length of me. It's the sexiest thing."

Plundering her mouth, he kissed her as if he hadn't just rocked her world. He wasn't pulling out, and she wondered why. Would this be it for them? One and done? She ran her fingers up his arms before burying them in the hair at the back of his neck. She claimed his mouth, enjoying the taste of him, the boldness of his tongue, all while bidding him farewell. If he never saw her again, she'd have this moment forever.

Chapter Eight

Tessa snuggled her backside against his groin, having drifted off minutes ago. It was around four in the morning, but sleep eluded Cam. He tightened his arm looped around her midriff, the weight of her breasts comforting him. Burying his face in her neck, he inhaled her scent, sneaking a kiss on her shoulder.

She overwhelmed him, drove him wild, and had done so without artifice and hidden motives. The memory of the best orgasm of his life lingered in his body and the goose-bumps forming on his skin. He'd felt her every touch, the brush of her lips across his chest, her fingers kneading his biceps, her short nails digging in his back. Her breathless sighs and gasps of pleasure echoed in his ears. What was this woman doing to him?

Seven days remained, and even if she'd let him have her daily, he wasn't sure that would be enough to rid his system of her. But did he want to? He took a moment to analyze what this emotion was. The one where holding her brought such joy. When seeing her smile had his heart leaping in his throat. The memory of being inside her competed with the day he'd earned his first million pounds.

He spent the remainder of the night formulating plans and tossing them aside. By the time her alarm went off, he hadn't settled on a single approach. But met with her sleepy gaze and grin, his grumpiness evaporated. He kissed her, nibbling on her ruby lips, splaying his fingers on her stomach, tempting him to lower it to her sex and truly make this a wonderful morning.

"Oh, no, you don't." She bolted off the couch and out of his arms. "I'll be late if you start that."

"Then be late." He leaned across to catch her hand.

"Promptness is a sign of respect." She danced out of his reach with a small chuckle.

He fell back, presented with her nudity as she hurried around his office, looking for her clothing. With her bustier on and her white shirt gaping, he imagined pressing her against the glass wall and burying himself in her. His cock twitched in anticipation.

"Keep prancing around like that, and you will be disrespectful," he said, his voice rough. He curled his fingers into fists, drew a shuddering breath in, then sat up. Her eyes widened, and her mouth parted on an 'oh.' He rested his forehead onto his palm, amazed she didn't know how sexy she was. If she ever decided to seduce him, he wouldn't stand a chance.

"My skirt?" she asked, and he looked up. She'd buttoned her shirt closed; the hem of it brushed against her upper thighs, hiding her sex from him.

"Closet." He gestured to where Marc had stashed them last night while she slept in Cam's arms.

Darting over, she opened doors until she found her skirts. She gasped, thumbed through the four others he'd had made for her, and stilled. Her shoulders stiffened, and her chin dropped to her chest.

"What's wrong?" He crossed the room and gripped her upper arms. She fought his tug, but when he insisted, she spun and buried her face against his chest, wrapping her arms around him, squeezing tight.

"Are these for me?" Her voice was husky, and he tilted her face up, one finger under her chin. Tears slid down her cheeks. She rubbed them, muffling a self-deprecating chuckle. "Thank you, Cam. It's a wonderful gesture."

"I couldn't remove the blood, but I had it dry-cleaned anyway." Such a small thing had an impact on her. It made him wonder if she didn't wear jewelry because she'd never known the joy of receiving it.

She wiped a cheek again before choosing a dark-brown floral skirt. She peeled it on under his watchful gaze, tucked her shirt in, and buckled on her belt.

"How's your thigh?" He pulled his jeans on, then the discarded T-shirt, and ran his fingers through his hair.

"Sore, but I'll live." She slipped her feet into her peep-toe shoes. Combing her hair with her fingers, she gathered the mass of hair over one shoulder. "Ready as I'll ever be."

"Anthony should be waiting downstairs. He'll take you to the publishers and bring you to me for lunch."

"Lunch?" She raised startled eyes to his, and a slow smile curled her lips. Her expectations were clear now; she'd thought he'd do her and walk away. He might have if she was any other woman.

"Oh, so you had no intention of taking me to lunch?" he teased. "Use my body and goodbye?"

Her eyes sparkled when she chuckled, shaking her head enough to send her hair flying. "A deal's a deal," she said. "Lunch is on me, but won't you need Anthony? I can take a taxi."

"Hell, no. He'll ensure you don't ditch me."

"Ditch you?" She laughed, crossing the room to brush her lips across his. "I wouldn't ditch you, not for a million dollars."

"Two?" he asked and received another headshake. "Ten?"

"Nope. You're priceless, Camden Mathews," she said.

Leaving him to retrieve her hotel card from her other skirt, she missed the expression he leveled on her. She had no idea how serious his question was. That she wouldn't forsake him no matter the incentive, left him lightheaded with a euphoric joy that rivaled the bliss of fucking her.

"I'll see you later, boss." Pressing another kiss to his lips, she left his office.

He sat, not caring on what. His world spun, his emotions spiraling out of control. He bounded up and settled behind his desk, going through last night's finances without focus. Giving up on understanding the numbers, he watched videos of her, instead.

A text from Watts had him staring at it, trying to assess how this news affected him. He'd analyze his tumultuous feelings later when his mind was clearer. Unexpected music intruded, and he tilted his head to listen. Entering the bathroom, he found Tessa's phone on the vanity. The name across the screen had the word 'publisher,' and he swiped to answer.

"Cam Mathews." He squashed the guilt he felt for taking the call on her behalf. She was looking forward to seeing the publisher, and if they canceled on her, there'd be hell to pay.

"Um, hello, I'm looking for Tessa du Toit," the woman said.

"This is Tessa's phone. Leave a message with me, and I'll get it to her."

"There's been an emergency, which is why I'm calling this early. Fiona would like to reschedule her eleven o'clock," she said.

"That won't suit me."

"I'm sorry, Mr. Mathews, but her son has a doctor's appointment at eleven-thirty." The woman's tone hardened. He didn't like the sound of that. It seemed 'hell' was on the horizon.

"Could Fiona see Tessa earlier?" he asked. Bringing the appointment forward meant Tessa wouldn't go hungry and would leave more of her day open to spending with him.

"Yes, if she could come in as soon as possible."

"She'll be there." He hung up, and after a quick shower, pulled on the spare clothing he kept in the office—a pair of black skinny jeans, a T-shirt, and a thigh-length black wool coat. Tying his shoelaces on his boots, he grabbed her phone, two helmets, and slipped the club's bike keys off the hook by the door. He chose not to wear his full safety gear, but with the time limit and the traffic, the bike was the quickest.

Within fifteen minutes, he parked the bike alongside Anthony, who climbed out of the car and nodded a greeting at Cam, clasping his hands in front of him.

"Check her out of the hotel and take her luggage to my place. I left her skirts at the office; fetch those too. Where are these publishers?"

Anthony rattled off the address as they strode into the hotel foyer. Cam headed for the manager, who scurried toward him.

"Mrs. du Toit is in the dining room, Mr. Mathews."

Watts's text had said a soon-to-be ex-Mrs. du Toit, but the manager didn't know that. The sweet spike of joy told Cam, at last, that her impending freedom delighted him.

"Thank you. My man will check her out." He gestured to Anthony before walking in the direction the manager had indicated.

Finding her was easy, a splash of color among the grays and blacks of the other patrons. Her hair was down, and she had run a brush through it. He took a moment to admire her in black ankle boots into tight black leggings with a colorful floral dress falling to mid-thigh.

He crossed the room, dodging people carrying plates of bacon and eggs. The second she saw him, her eyes widened, then narrowed as she ran a heated gaze over him. Lust slammed into him, snatching his breath. Her mouth parted for the tip of her tongue to push on her upper lip. She mouthed his name.

"Morning." He nodded at Owen. "You left your phone." He didn't offer it to her since it didn't look like she had pockets. "I answered it when the publishers called. They need to see you now."

"Now?" She rose, splaying her hands on top of the table. Gasping, her cheeks paled, and her fingers twitched. "But—"

"Anthony is checking you out and taking care of your luggage."

"Thank the Lord for Anthony." She chuckled. "Cam, this is Owen." The man held out his hand for a shake, which Cam accepted. "Have a wonderful trip, Owen-babe, and I'll see you back at the office." Her colleague rose to hug her, whispering words in her ear that bloomed a smile across her lips.

"A pleasure to meet you, Cam," he said.

Cam nodded, offered a helmet to her, and she fell into step beside him, coming to a standstill alongside his bike.

"She's a beauty." After tugging her helmet on, she tilted her head back, silently asking him to tighten the strap. He did so then pulled on his helmet. Swinging a leg over the bike, he started it and waited for her to slide on. When she did, she showed no fear and placed her feet with ease as if familiar with motorcycles. She wrapped her arms around his waist, giving a squeeze to say she was ready.

He shook his head. There had to be something bad about her, something he didn't like because so far, she was perfect. He swerved through traffic, dodging cars, and cyclists. Not once did she complain. She leaned when he did with her hips snug against his backside. Sad the ride was over, he parked the bike outside the publisher's building. Tomorrow or the next day, he'd take her on a lunch run somewhere.

She swung a leg off and stepped onto the paving, fiddling with the helmet's clasp. Through the visor, her eyes sparkled, showing her enjoyment. He undid the buckle and left her to remove the helmet while he hurried to undo his own. Looping it over the handlebars, he circled an arm around her waist and yanked her against him.

"I want to kiss you." He drowned in her chocolate eyes.

"I'm not stopping you." She grinned, placing her free hand on his bicep.

The taste of her was ambrosia, he decided a moment later. Her petal-soft lips and the tremor rippling through him combined to shred his control. He drew away, holding her close with a trembling hand on her hip.

"Seventh floor." He took the helmet from her and grabbed his before ushering her into the building. His reputation served them well when they rode the elevator up a minute later. The security had taken one look at him, checked Tessa's name was on the roster, and let them through.

"Mr. Mathews," the receptionist gasped, and Tessa laughed, wiggling her eyebrows at him. He found himself grinning, his gaze traveling her face to linger on her kiss-swollen lips.

"Tessa du Toit to see Fiona." He spread his legs to accommodate his erection and to imply he had no intention of waiting any longer than he had to.

"Yes, right this way." The flustered woman gestured to Tessa to follow.

She hesitated, shooting a nervous glance at him. He smiled in encouragement, and she nodded, drew a deep breath in then trailed the woman to an office door. He balanced the helmets on the reception seating and faced the window, watching the foot traffic below. He didn't expect the meeting to take long. After all, Fiona was pressed for time.

If she declined to represent Tess, he'd publish her books. It would mean seeing more of her, and for him, that was a win-win. The door opened, and she stepped through, her cheeks flushed and her eyes gleaming. She bounced with happiness as she rushed over to him. She raised her arms to hug him but lowered them before doing so.

"Cam, this is Fiona." She introduced the blonde next to her, a woman in her mid-thirties in jeans and a blouse.

He offered his hand for a shake. "Thank you for seeing Tessa sooner, and I'm sorry about your son."

"Suggesting an earlier appointment was genius. I knew Tessa had flown in from South Africa, but I didn't know what her travel arrangements were." She turned to Tess. "I'll send through the contract. Once you're happy with it, sign it, and we'll start the process. Welcome to the family."

Cam dug his wallet out of his back pocket and held out his lawyer's card. "Email it through to Dennis; he'll take a look at it."

"But..." Tessa clasped his forearm. He flashed her a smile, and she returned a tentative one. "We'll talk about this later, Mr. Take-charge."

"Yes, ma'am." He ushered her into the elevator. "Congratulations."

"Oh." She grinned but gave him a shrug. "I'll get excited when I sign."

"Why so cautious?"

"I'm scared it will be snatched from me. That would break my heart." She raised her big brown eyes to his, revealing her fear. With his heart threatening to explode, he longed to tug her into his arms. How could a mature woman be so childlike?

"We'll find you another publisher." Like him.

She huffed. "You say that like it's easy, Cam. This took me nineteen months."

"You have me now." Little did she realize how serious he was.

She gaped. "No. It's all me or not at all, and I told you, I don't abuse my friends. As it is, I owe you for the lawyer."

"Buy me lunch tomorrow, and we'll call it quits."

She snorted, but a smile teased her lips. Unable to resist her any longer, he snatched a kiss, stepping forward until her back bumped against the elevator's wall. He kissed her hard, clinging to her lips in the brief time he had. When the ping announced they'd reached their destination, it tore a growl from him.

Chapter Nine

Pressed against the side of an elevator was a position Tessa had never imagined finding herself in. The combined fragrance of his cologne and heated skin smothered her. She basked in it, loving the need flooding her body, loosening her limbs. His lips demanded a response from her, and she was happy to oblige him. He couldn't know how his kisses robbed her of breath and escalated her heartbeat until a fluttering consumed her chest. Her hairline tingled when she imagined explaining to him what he did to her.

The elevator dinged, and a part of her was grateful for it. When he growled in protest, she threw out her hand to grip the mirror, her knees shaking. She'd never heard anything as sexy and as debilitating as the sound that vibrated up his throat. He offered her the helmet, then laced his fingers through hers when his hand was free. A tug and she stumbled after him. But instead of heading for the bike, he aimed for the coffee shop across the road.

She allowed a smile to form. Any man wanting to impress her had to know she loved coffee, cafés, and the aroma of roasted beans. He chose a booth along the street front, placing his helmet on the seat between him and the glass. Before meeting his gaze, she did the same. She was grinning like the Cheshire Cat, and despite the women ogling him, she was too delighted to be here with him to care.

"Love coffee?" he teased, his top lip curling in that devastating way of his. Just the sight of it sent a tremble through her.

"Yes, thank you for bringing me here." She drew in a deep breath to calm her nerves and to inhale the aroma of brewed coffee, as much as her lungs could hold.

When the waitress came around, she gave her order to Cam before watching the foot traffic rushing past the café. A man stared at her, and she flashed him a polite smile, in case their gazes met by accident. He didn't respond but shifted his attention to Cam. Malevolence saturated his stiff posture and lethal glare.

She took a second to study him. He was tall, broad-shouldered, filling out his storm-gray coat with ease. Dark hair brushed across his temple when the wind tossed it. She couldn't see the color of his eyes, but overall, he was handsome in an ominous way.

"Do you know that man, Cam?" She gestured out the window. "He's staring at you."

Cam glanced outside and scowled, deep grooves marring his temple. "Yes, that's Logan."

With a muttered curse, he bounded out of the chair and the café. He burst across the pavement, striding toward the man, his fists at his side. Logan straightened off the car, facing Cam without fear. Was this the same Logan Cam mentioned yesterday? She'd ask him later when they were once more alone.

Her almond milk cappuccino slid in front of her, distracting her, and she formed a grateful smile for the waitress. Shooting a glance at Cam, she poured one sugar into her mug and stirred. Logan yelled something; the red on his cheeks and clenched fists said he was furious. He grabbed Cam by the shoulder then punched him in the stomach. Cam doubled over, but when he didn't respond, it looked like he had no intention of retaliating. Behind them, a car's doors opened, and two men stepped out, flanking Logan. A dart of fear dropped into her stomach and curdled there. They outnumbered Cam three to one.

Going on instinct, she rushed outside. The door closing behind her with a scraping noise announced her presence. Logan glanced at her, but she ignored him, approaching their party to hover behind Cam. She shot calculating glances at the two bodyguards, wondering how best to take them down. This was going to hurt, again.

Cam faced her, towering over her. He released his hold on his stomach to grab her elbows. Pain creased his eyes, and she had to admit; she was ready to pummel Logan for punching him. "Tessa, please, go inside. I don't need you injured again."

"I'm not leaving you." She peered around him. "What do they want?"

"It's a misunderstanding," he said with a stiff, dismissive shrug and a wince.

"It is not," Logan roared. "Impregnating my sister isn't a misunderstanding, Cam."

"For the love of it, Logan, I never touched her." Cam faced him.

"She claims otherwise." Logan folded his arms across his chest, stiffening his suit jacket.

"Paternity test anyone?" Tessa stepped around Cam to lower her ass onto a nearby bicycle stand. It wasn't comfortable, but she wanted a relaxed stance to defuse the situation. When she'd slipped around Cam, he'd trailed his hand across her stomach as if to prevent her from endangering herself. Short of yanking her into the café, she wasn't about to abandon him.

"We considered it, but Gina had a miscarriage, so that option isn't possible," Logan said, his tone laced with hatred, anger, and filial helplessness.

"Did you see the blood?" This was a personal discussion, but Tessa wanted to know whether Gina had truly lost the baby or meant to deceive her brother. It was known to happen. One only had to watch a soap opera to learn how to fake a miscarriage.

"What? No." Paling, Logan gaped at her, like the thought hadn't occurred to him.

Cam's eyes widened, which meant he cared for Gina regardless of this scheme she may or may not have concocted. Tessa wasn't sure why she believed him innocent. Perhaps it was because she needed to think he was a good guy. Not that it should matter when she'd fly out of his life soon enough.

"Listen, it's not like in the movies. Miscarriages are messy. Blood would saturate her bed linen, the carpet, the bathroom, wherever she said it happened. I hope you took her to the hospital?" Tessa met Logan's eyes with an arched brow. This close, they were a lovely dove gray. "The gynae needs to take a look to make sure she's fine and that children are possible in the future."

By Logan's pinched lips, she knew she'd struck home. Hopping off the stand, she returned to Cam's side. He looped an arm around her, a smile teasing his lips and gratitude warming his eyes. Not that she'd intervened for that. She just couldn't bear to see Logan punch him again.

"I expect you'll need to apologize to Cam when all is said and done." She leaned into his embrace to press a kiss to his upper arm. "Thank you for not punching him in the mouth. I'm partial to his kisses."

Cam grunted and tightened his arm around her. "Let me know if you need anything, Logan." He steered her into the café, his hand at the base of her spine. "Please tell me you didn't suffer through a miscarriage?"

"No, I'm a writer. I research random topics, but I feel for those who've gone through such a trauma. It's unfair for women to pretend to miscarry when so many others have suffered."

He gestured to the waitress, and she removed their cold coffees. Tessa frowned. She would've drunk it like that because asking for another round when it was their fault they grew cold, meant she felt obligated to pay for both orders.

"Thank you, Tess-luv," Cam said, drawing her attention.

She shrugged, fighting the sudden urge to dip her chin to her chest. "I'd love to be a fly on the wall when Logan asks her to visit the gynecologist. Never a pleasant trip."

Cam flashed a stiff smile that didn't reach his blue eyes. There was seriousness in his assessing gaze, like something momentous had occurred to him.

She reached across the table and grabbed his hand. "What's wrong?"

"I—"

The waitress placed their coffees onto the table, forcing Tessa to release him. She did so, cupping her mug with trembling fingers. Tension filled the air, thick enough to snatch her breath and spike her heart rate. She added sugar to her fresh cappuccino and stirred, keeping her gaze on his face.

"You didn't believe I was capable of doing this?" His voice was hoarse, and the grip on his espresso whitened his knuckles.

"No."

He clenched his jaw, and a pulse ticked in his neck.

Concerned, she allowed the emotion to pull her lips down. What had she said to offend him? He looked furious, his posture stiff.

"I'm sorry, was I supposed to believe Logan?" She shook her head. "Even if you command me to, I won't. You don't strike me as the type of man to abandon his child." She sipped her cappuccino before meeting his swirling blue gaze again. "Besides, it shouldn't matter what I think."

He scowled, said no more, and was content to sit there with his shoulders slumped and his head lowered in misery.

She hid a chuckle behind her mug. Men could be emotional sometimes. If he chose to explain his mood swing, then she'd listen, but she wasn't going to pry. She enjoyed her coffee in silence, staring at the people rushing past the window. He didn't fill the silence, so she didn't make the effort to either. At one point, he excused himself. Not thinking anything about it, she finished her coffee with a sad sigh, having relished every sip.

"Ready?" he asked, not sliding onto his seat.

"Yes, let's get the bill."

"I've taken care of it." He grabbed his helmet and offered her a hand.

She accepted, placing hers into his warm calloused one. His grip tightened while she shuffled across the seat. When she made to release him, he drew her closer for a quick kiss.

With a frown, she met his gaze. "Will you tell me what's bothering you?" She pried when she'd planned not to.

"Yes, but not here."

She nodded, slipped her hand free, and retrieved her helmet. Following him to the bike, he kept his stride shorter, so she wouldn't have to run after him. That was considerate of him, and she flashed him a grateful smile when they reached the motorcycle. He hooked his helmet over the handlebar and turned to loop his arm around her waist, yanking her snugly against him. He cupped her cheeks, burying his fingers in her hair.

This kiss curled her toes, with her internal organs doing some sort of line dance. Giddiness and excitement skittered along her nerve endings and tingled her scalp. He pulled away, returning to brush his lips across hers, to inhale her breath. He caressed her hair out of her face with trembling fingers, and passion lingered in his eyes.

"Shall we?" he asked.

"Where to?" She stepped away to tug her helmet on, lifting her chin for assistance.

Hesitating, his hands stilled under her chin. "Home." He watched her, waiting for her reaction as if he dreaded it.

"Sure," she said, and he released a deep sigh. For all she knew, he needed to change or to fetch something. Going to his home shouldn't have such importance. "I'm not agreeing to be your hostage, am I?"

The corners of his eyes crinkled, and she thought she heard him chuckle. "I'm tempted, but no."

She threw her leg over the bike behind him and wrapped her arms around his waist. As he meandered through London traffic, she wondered about his unexpected seriousness, his mood fluctuations, and the importance of her being in his home. Well, since she was with him until after lunch, then he could act whatever way he wanted to, because, in two to three hours, it was farewell.

Chapter Ten

Cam felt as if Logan had punched him in the head. Words, images, emotions spun, increasing in speed and potency until nausea roiled in the pit of his stomach. What the hell had happened? One moment, the standing argument over Gina reared its head again, the usual punch thrown. He understood, having known Logan since school. The man was frustrated, angry, scared; Gina's 'situation' twisting his heart, confusing him.

The next moment, Tessa had spoken logic into the middle of the months-old feud. She'd rushed out of the café to defend him, her coiled posture reminiscent of last night. That she didn't consider him capable of impregnating Gina ripped a hole through his heart, now vulnerable to an icy wind of truth funneling through it. She'd sat sipping her coffee, unaware of her impact on his thoughts, her calm presence shaking his understanding of his world.

She clung to him as he zipped through traffic. It felt…right, having her behind him and coming home with him. He was an idiot. This was temporary, what was between them. Soon, she'd walk away, board a plane, and live a life excluding him. There it was. That sharp pain gripped his chest, squeezing until he couldn't breathe.

He didn't want her to leave him. Watts's text said she was in for a divorce, and if Cam could spare her the pain, he would. But she'd be free. A lump formed in his throat, and he struggled to swallow past it. She'd be free to be his?

He drove the bike into the underground level of his block of luxury flats. The cooler temperature drew him back to the moment. Once she entered his home, she'd see her luggage, then what? Would she become angry? Laugh it off? Make plans anyway? Thank him for Anthony's consideration?

He scowled, hating not knowing how she might react. How did he want her to? Strip right there and let him bend her over his leather couch? He hardened at the thought, beaming with eagerness. He flicked out the bike stand. The cooling engine tinkled. She climbed off and offered her chin; a sweet smile revealed when she flipped her visor back.

"I've never ridden a Ducati before." She slid the helmet off after he unbuckled her clasp.

"What are you used to?" He laced his fingers through hers. They held their helmets as he summoned the elevator.

"Triumphs. Forest has a dislike for Harley. Says they're too expensive for what you get." The door pinged, and she stepped inside first.

Cam followed, pressing the button for the top floor.

"You both have good taste." Leaning against the side of the elevator, he ran an admiring gaze over her.

He wanted to remember her, the curve of her hip, the bounce to her breasts, the stubborn tilt to her chin, and the excited sparkle in her brown eyes. The elevator opened onto his penthouse apartment, and he gestured to her to lead the way. She did, gasping at the wall of glass windows revealing London's cityscape.

She walked past her bags, placed the helmet on his kitchen counter, and opened his fridge.

"We can order in." He set his helmet alongside hers.

"Pizza," she said, her words mumbled with cherry tomatoes in her hand and one halfway to her mouth. "I wish. Chinese?"

"Whatever you want." He leaned his backside against the counter and crossed his legs at the ankles. Gripping the counter's edge, he waited. Any moment now, she'd mention leaving him, visiting her friends, and he hadn't yet decided how he'd respond.

"I'll need my phone. I promised to let Owen know about the publishers."

He took it out of his jacket pocket and left it in the wooden fruit bowl he used for his many sets of keys.

"Okay, out with it. Why are you so tense?" She arched a brow as she popped in another tomato.

"Your luggage," he said.

"Yes, what about them? They look intact, and I doubt Anthony would trash them."

"They're in my home, Tessa." Cam stepped forward to grab her hips. She peered at him, holding one tomato to her lips while she chewed. "Where I want them to stay."

Her eyes widened, and her chewing paused. Holding up a finger, she swallowed. "You want me to bunk with you?" She gestured with a tomato to his apartment.

He nodded.

"But I promised Naomi and Emily I'd stay with them."

"Plans change." He wrapped his lips around the tomato, stealing it from her.

"You're serious?" She shook her head, cascading her hair around her. "I couldn't intrude. I've known you for two days, Cam."

"I have a gym, a laundry room, a massive telly, and a housekeeper who'll buy whatever ingredients you need for your salads."

She laughed, throwing her head back in wild abandonment. "Holy cow, Cam. All you had to do was ask nicely. I don't need you to bribe me."

"I want you in my arms, my home, and my bed. Please stay, Tessa." Silence met his request, her gaze darting over his face. What she saw he couldn't say, but this close to her, he wanted to sip at her pink lips, to bury his nose and inhale the fragrance of her hair.

"Bloody hell. Don't ever use those gorgeous blue eyes on me again. I'd buy a used car from you."

"Is that a yes?" He looped his arms around her and crushed her against him.

"Can we order in groceries?" she asked instead of answering him. Twisting to place the half-eaten container of tomatoes on the counter, she grasped his cheeks, gave him a sweet kiss, and said, "and while we wait for the delivery, you show me your home?"

The pleasure bursting through him coated his chest with a euphoric warmth that had him grinning at her, wide enough to make his cheeks ache. "Woman, you undo me." He ignored the overt rasp of his voice.

She stilled, fear, longing, and sadness darkening her eyes. "Cam, you can't become involved with me, us, not emotionally. What if I'm still married? What if I grow to care for you? Leaving you would kill me." She lowered her gaze, not before he saw the shimmer on her lashes.

"We live these last days with no thoughts of the future, Tessa."

"That's irresponsible," she said with a scowl, lifting her gaze to meet his.

"Doing stupid things is how you lose yourself in London." He stepped back to tick off points on his fingers. "Nightclub brawl? Check. Find a publisher? Check. Beguile sexy club owner? Check."

"Beguile?" She giggled.

"Seduce?"

"I didn't, did I?" Shock dropped her jaw and parted her tempting lips.

"Enchant?"

"Yup, African witchcraft at its finest," she said.

He chuckled then wrapped her in his arms for a long hug. "Let's place the order, then the fun can begin."

"Fun?" She snorted. "A salad takes half an hour to make."

"While we wait for the ingredients, we can have fun." He flashed his most charming smile.

"If by fun, you mean strip and bend me over that couch, then, hell yes."

His breath hitched, and he dug his fingers in her hips. How had she known he longed to do that? He pressed a hard kiss to her lips before stepping away and running a trembling hand through his hair.

"Give me a list," he said.

She picked up her phone, unlocked it, and placed a shopping list on a notes app before him. From his phone, he messaged Hayley, his housekeeper, trusting her to get the best. Then he could abduct Tessa to his room without having to listen for the intercom.

"Done." He pocketed his phone and grabbed her hand.

"That quickly?" she asked.

He ignored her question. "This is the gym," he said, tugging her past the opened door. He didn't pause, and she gave a breathless giggle when she hurried after his long strides. "Guest room which you won't see the inside of." He gestured to the closed door to the right. "Laundry room." He entered his bedroom and closed the door behind her. "My room and yours for the next week."

"Is that so?" Her eyes sparkled.

"Strip or so help me, I'll tear your clothes off you."

"Wow. I have my bank card somewhere. I'll pay to see that." She patted herself down as if she searched her non-existent pockets.

"Tessa." He lowered his voice, conveying his sincerity.

She chuckled and dropped onto the side of his bed to undo her bootlaces. For a moment, he was torn. Should he undress as well and miss seeing her remove each item one at a time? Or should he watch her and worry about his state of dress later?

She shimmied out of her tights, tossing them over his clotheshorse. When she gripped the hem of her dress, he burst forward, forcing her to fall backward onto the bed. With an eagerness he hadn't felt since his youth, he crawled over her until his lips met hers.

Chapter Eleven

Kissing his cheek, Tessa nuzzled his neck, brushed her lips down his throat before dropping her head onto his chest. Her limbs were languid, in a semi-paralysis from the best treatment he'd given her to date. Her body hummed with contentment. Her soul soared in jubilation. It was short-lived, but she wouldn't bemoan that. He'd said to live each day without regrets, and she would.

"Now, can I eat?" Following the trail of a tattoo, she twirled a pattern across his skin. Goosebumps formed under her touch, summoning a laugh.

"Shower first, then I can patch your thigh while you prepare this amazing salad," he said. Scowling, she pushed up to look at him. She pouted, not wanting to wait another minute to eat something. He chuckled, his fingers pinching her chin for a playful tug. "Two minutes; hop to it. I'll check if the food's arrived."

"Fine," she said, then ruined her petulance with a giggle. "I'll obey, but only because your kisses make my knees weak."

"Oh, do they?" He flashed his charming smile, the one that dimpled his cheek.

With his blue eyes turning smoky, she saw a future without food looming before her and darted into the bathroom lest he tested out his knee-weakening kisses.

Minutes later in one of his T-shirts, she padded on bare feet to the kitchen. He had the fridge door open as he unpacked salad ingredients, placing them on the counter. In low-riding yoga pants and nothing else, he looked hot enough to photograph for the latest GQ. With all that caramel skin on display, she was tempted to skip her salad and lick him instead.

Her stomach growled in protest.

He'd set out the other items she needed. Olive oil, a variety of spices, and garlic, which she'd forgo if she wanted any more of his kisses.

A chopping board awaited her, and she stood in front of it, pressing a hand to her gurgling abdomen. The aroma of pizza reached her, and she grinned at the box on the island. She ran her fingers over the kale leaves as he looped his arms around her from behind to kiss her shoulder.

"My shirt?" he asked.

"Yes. I hope you don't mind. I'll do laundry later, including this." She picked up the knife and sliced into the pepper, biting off the end of it.

"I don't mind." He slid his fingers down her waist, over her hips to hook the hem. He yanked upward, and she wiggled her backside to dislodge him, a smothered giggle escaping her.

"Food first, please. I might need two meals a day if you keep this up," she said around another bite of pepper.

"I'd advise it." He dropped onto his haunches, his fingers gripping her thigh. "Let's take a look." He unclipped the wet bandage and unwound it, nudging her thighs apart with his knuckles. Then he peeled the gauze off and sighed.

"Bad? Good?" She twisted to look at him.

"Stand still," he said, gesturing to her to face forward, then he lifted the shirt to place a kiss on her bare butt cheek. He jumped up and disappeared, returning with a first aid box. On his knees again, he treated her wound before wrapping a bandage around it.

"Good then?" She sliced cucumber between bites.

"No bleeding; no loose stitches." He placed the box on the island.

Circling his arms around her again, he rested his chin on her shoulder and watched her prepare the salad. He cupped her hips again, then ran one hand lower, hooked his shirt, and lifted it, brushing her inner thigh upward.

"Cam." She wished she didn't have the urge to spread her thighs to grant him easier access. Come tomorrow, she wouldn't be able to walk without looking like John Wayne.

"Tessa," he growled, just as he dipped his fingers between her legs, hitting the spot that had her gasping.

She trembled. A throaty moan soon followed when his dexterous fingers tormented her. His phone rang, and she whimpered, needing him to ignore it, but he didn't.

Keeping his touch there, he reached back and picked up the call. "Speak."

She expected him to step away, to deal with the person on the line, but he didn't. He flicked his fingers, drawing a smothered purr from her. She threw back her head and spread her thighs like the tart he'd called her. As long as he didn't stop, she didn't care.

Trembling, everything within her stilled on the cusp of an exquisite orgasm; she threw herself off the edge, thrashed as whimper after whimper escaped her clenched lips.

"You're so sexy," he whispered, then nipped her earlobe, sending fresh shivers down her spine. "Yes, I'm on my way." He placed his phone on the counter and crushed her against him when he kissed her neck. "I'll leave Anthony for you if you want to visit your friends."

She spun and cupped his cheeks, feathering her fingers over his lips. "Business?"

He nodded, snatched a hard kiss, and disappeared down the passage. She assumed he had to dress into something a little more appropriate. As she sliced an avocado, she nodded, admitting he'd spoiled her with his attention. He was a busy man, and he'd spared her many hours of his time. Besides, the distance now would help when she left London. Rinsing her fingers, she wiped her hands on a kitchen towel and unlocked her phone. She'd send a text to Emily and see if she was free tonight.

Down the passage, his boots thumped on the pale-blonde wooden flooring. She opened the pizza and grabbed a slice, offering it to him. His smile was more beautiful than all of him in his tight blue jeans, a black T-shirt, and a biker's jacket. She'd never tell him, though. Within a minute, the slice was gone, so she offered him another one before closing the box.

"I'll leave these in the oven in case you're hungry later." She slid the box in, closing the oven door with a snap.

"I should stay." He looped his arms around her. "I want to stay."

"Business first, or else they'll call again. Just...be safe." She bit her lip, wondering at the potent emotions exploding in her chest. Shit, she knew that feeling. She wanted to spend every waking moment with him, many hours with him buried inside her, bask in the sunlight of his smiles, wallow in the safety of his arms.

"What's wrong?" He cupped her cheek to peer into her eyes.

"Alarm code for when I leave?" She nudged her head at the white box on the wall. He told her then gave her a sweet, sensual, and breath-stealing kiss.

"When I get back, we'll discuss why you won't tell me what's wrong." He scooped up his helmet and strolled out of the apartment.

65

Chapter Twelve

Familiar brown hair cascaded over a beloved face, obscuring her crystalline blue eyes. Tessa grinned at Emily. The long-awaited reunion had taken seventeen years to organize. Seeing her best friend from her childhood had brought back so many memories. Energy pulsed through her like she was young and rejuvenated, while at the same time, every lived year resonated in her 'ancient' bones. So much time had passed. Her husband, Kyle, had greeted her but had left them alone for the most part.

It was growing late, so the sight through Emily's lounge window of a sleek black car had Tessa leaping to kiss her friend goodnight. They'd planned to meet again for coffee, so a protracted farewell wasn't necessary. Anthony didn't climb out of the car to open for her. That didn't alarm her, but the man stepping out did.

Logan.

She stopped two meters away, searching the street for his goons or Anthony. "What do you want?" When one of his men climbed out the front of the car to flank him, she leapt back.

"Coffee." Logan folded his arms across his chest, drawing his suit tight over his broad shoulders.

"I'm not going anywhere with you." She lowered her handbag to the ground and toed off her flats.

He frowned, staring at her toes for a minute before meeting her gaze. "I'm not going to hurt you, Tessa. I'd like to thank you for today."

"Send flowers." She didn't care if he thought her rude.

"Just get in the bloody car," he said, his voice abrasive.

"I watch crime shows. Going anywhere with you is certain death."

He glowered at her and gestured with two fingers at his man, who lunged at her. *Shit.* He was tall, way over six feet. She had few options on how to survive this. One was surprise, for a start. Bursting forward, she shortened the distance. She redirected his grasping hand, used his knee as leverage, and vaulted into the air to deliver a swift punch to his throat. Not hard enough to kill him, but it would incapacitate him while he gasped for air. She landed beside him as he stumbled to his knees.

"I said no, Logan." She returned to her bag, keeping a distance between him and his man.

"Fuck, did you kill him?" Logan unfolded his arms to drop limply at his sides. The scowl he leveled on her was intimidating, but she wasn't going to let him bully her.

"No. Now, leave or tell me what you want, and none of this thank-you nonsense."

"*Elysium*," he gritted out between clenched teeth.

She rolled her eyes and threw her hands into the air. This again? "They attacked Bart with knives."

"I've dealt with them. This is something more. My father lost ownership of the club to Cam's father in a poker game. It's the last thing he owned before he died."

"So, offer to buy it." She shrugged, not understanding what *Elysium* had to do with her.

Logan gave her a look implying he'd tried that avenue. "Cam won't sell for the same reason."

"Then why come after me?"

"He cares for you," Logan said.

"A barter based on perceived affection?" She laughed while shaking her head at his stupidity. "I'm his tart for six more days, then it's farewell for life. Besides, you know Cam better than I do. He'd come after you rather than give into your demands."

A car pulled up behind Logan's, and Anthony hopped out, rushing toward her with angry strides. He was a wonderful sight, shooting warning glances at Logan before falling into place beside her. Thank goodness Kyle hadn't come out to use a few of his ex-bouncer moves, not with his bad back. And she didn't want to endanger Emily with this silliness.

"You're not injured, are you?" Anthony appraised her, searching for injuries.

"I'm fine, Anthony. Logan just wanted a chat."

Logan raised his hands as if to surrender before gathering his man and returning to his car. Only when the sleek vehicle disappeared did she allow her shoulders to relax. Scooping up her bag, she slid her shoes on and gave Anthony a sweet smile.

"You know what this means, right?" he asked while escorting her to the car with a hand on her elbow. "Double the security, or you stay in the apartment."

"House arrest?" She gaped. "Do we have to tell Cam?"

Anthony nodded before he slammed the door.

"Shit," she said to the empty car moments before he slipped into the driver's seat.

The doors locked, and the window between him and her closed. He'd assumed she'd try to convince him not to blab to Cam, and she would have. Thwarted, she spent the ride grumbling to herself and practicing what she'd say to Cam. It wasn't as if Logan had threatened her, nor had she truly been in danger.

"Anthony, please," she asked when he opened the door.

"It's done, Mrs. du Toit." His tone was all business and final.

She marched ahead, giving him the cold shoulder. He could bloody well stay in the foyer, and she said as much when the elevator arrived. Stepping into the apartment's minimal lighting and the breathtaking view of London greeting her, she mumbled to herself about men in general. The panoramic cityscape didn't calm her. Minutes later, she found appeasement punching and kicking Cam's boxing bag until sweat trickled down her spine, and her knuckles glowed red.

~*~

Cam stepped through the door, panic gripping his chest and squeezing tight. The blood on his hands and T-shirt mattered not. Anthony's text had shifted his axis, where slicing off a man's finger was no longer a priority. Ensuring Tessa's safety was.

"What the fuck?" Logan asked when Cam dropped his closest bodyguard, uncaring that the fresh blood on his hand was his own. "I wouldn't have denied you entry."

"Stay away from Tessa." Cam slammed his palms on Logan's mahogany desk.

"So, you *do* care." Logan smirked. "She seems to think you're short-term. What happens after six days, Cam? Put her on a plane and forget the bliss you've found between her legs?"

Red tinged Cam's vision, and he leapt back, clenching and unclenching his fists, trying to restrain the need to punch his best friend in the face.

"Perhaps I could sway her to my side?"

"You can try." It was Cam's turn to smirk. *Not for ten million dollars*, she'd said.

"Her voice, her accent—"

"Yes, I care." Cam didn't want to hear what Logan thought of her. Tessa was his, and it would remain that way. "Using a woman to force me to sell *Elysium* is low, even for you." He ran a bloody hand over his face, bone-weary with this unnecessary drama. "I tell you what. I'll talk to her about the club, and if she says to sell it, then so be it."

Logan's breath caught with the hope on his face breaking into a genuine smile, one Cam hadn't seen in a while.

"I'll tell you her decision once she boards her plane."

"Fair enough," Logan said.

Cam grunted and left, climbing onto his bike with his thoughts brushing the surface of his red-hazed mind. Any deeper would reveal his emotions, would demand he beg her to stay with him. He didn't give a damn about *Elysium*. Because of Gina's deception and Logan's unwavering belief Cam had hurt his sister, he'd been belligerent about it.

He strode into his apartment and paused, not surprised to find Tessa awake. She was at his dining table, typing away on her keyboard. Her reading glasses hid her eyes from him.

"Fuck," he said, instant arousal spiking sharp need through his core. She looked like a librarian.

"Since you didn't stumble in, I'm going to assume that's not your blood." She typed as she spoke, then pushed away from the table.

"What are you wearing?" He fought the chuckle rumbling up his chest and failed. She looked like a pink Teletubby in fleece overalls. A thick braid fell over one shoulder.

"It's a onesie," she said, taking his leather jacket from his fingers and draping it across the kitchen counter. His helmet followed suit, then she tugged his shirt off him.

"I like the zip." He trailed a blood-stained fingertip from her chin to her pelvis.

"Are you partial to this shirt?" She peered at him through her glasses. "If we bleach then burn it, forensics can't trace the source."

"It's just a finger," he said. "I didn't kill him, but I didn't stay, not when I heard you were in danger." He gripped her shoulders, stilling her.

"I asked him not to tell you." She rested her temple on his chest with her fingers at his bare waist.

"Logan promised not to bother you again."

"You saw him? Alone?" Her lips clenched white when Cam nodded.

"I struck a deal. I'd let you decide *Elysium's* fate."

"Me?" She laughed. "My loyalty lies with you. What a fool he is."

"He believes you'll be fair." Cam pulled away to wash his hands in the sink.

She searched the cupboards until she found bleach. Handing him a towel, she nudged him out of the way with her hip then poured bleach and water into the sink. Using a steel spatula, she pressed the shirt and towel in.

"This isn't necessary." He looped his arms around her fleece-covered body. "Hayley knows what to do."

"This happens often?" Tessa twisted to look at him.

"More than I'd like. Since my father's death, I've had to solidify my position. Most saw me as a playboy, incapable of sustaining his empire. I'm steering it toward legal enterprises since dodging the law is tiresome. Still, a few require a more violent approach." He captured her lips with his. "When we were kids, Logan and I made a pact to leave this all behind us."

"Are you mafia?" She wrapped her arms around him with her hands splaying across his shoulder blades.

He took that as a sign of acceptance. It mattered to him what she thought. "My origins are, and I'll always be in danger. Some cling to the old ways."

"Just as long as you don't die on me in the next six days, after that, I wouldn't know." She burrowed into him, her embrace tightening.

Silence permeated the kitchen, spreading through the apartment. He scowled, not wanting to think about her leaving or his life afterward.

"Let's get you out of this thing," he said.

"No, you shower while I finish the chapter. I must write when my muse is eager." She tugged, and he released her, trailing reluctant fingers across her hip.

"Shower?" He raised his arm to sniff his armpit.

"Yes. The stench of salt and iron clung to his pores, announcing his evening spent in the bowels of London." She pushed her glasses up with her forefinger.

He grinned, kissed her neck, and headed for his room. "Fifteen minutes, then your muse had better be less eager."

Chapter Thirteen

THE SECOND THE SHOWER came on, Tessa was free to react, gripping the table, her knuckles white. As her thoughts spiraled out of control, she struggled to breathe, to remain calm. She should've known he was too good to be true. There had to be something about him that wasn't perfect. But, dammit, why could he not pick his nose or have a foot fetish? Anything was better than a stone-cold killer.

All right, she wasn't being fair. He'd said he was trying to leave it all behind him, yet some poor bastard had lost a finger tonight. He hadn't taken their life, but that didn't mean mutilation was acceptable. She jumped up to pace, alternating between wringing her hands or throwing them in wide arcs as she debated with her internal voice.

Could she leave without angering him? And if she did, would he hunt her, demand a finger? Would it not be safer to remain here and leave as planned? Could she sleep with him like nothing had changed? She thought of his sculpted torso and beautiful blue eyes, and that familiar spark exploded into a blaze. Yes, she still wanted him. She cursed her body, acknowledging the tingles in her nethers and her pebbled nipples. Tonight had knocked him off the pedestal, and in a way, that wasn't a bad thing.

She stepped onto the balcony, relishing the crisp air on her flushed cheeks. Sucking in great gulps of air, she allowed it to cool her panic. Before her, the River Thames meandered like an obsidian snake, glimmering in the moonlight and reflecting the golden glow of Tower Bridge. Despite the beautiful view, her thoughts ricocheted. He hadn't hurt her, and she doubted he'd show any unkindness toward her. Was she talking herself into staying?

Turning her gaze inward, she focused on the feelings he invoked. Lust was expected, but she was also fond of him. Too fond. Discovering the darker side to him hadn't changed how she felt. She'd miss him, that was for sure.

His warmth at her back had her straightening seconds before he ran his hands from her hips to her belly. He tugged her against the length of him. His just-showered scent engulfed her, and she inhaled, hoping to memorize it. He placed a kiss on her head as he unzipped her and slipped a hand inside the gaping onesie. She moaned when he cupped a breast, brushing across her nipple with tantalizing slowness. Yes, she was his tart. She readily admitted it.

"Is your muse done with you?" he asked, his voice hoarse. He nipped her ear, and she writhed in his arms. His teeth sent shards of delicious pleasure skittering to the ends of her body.

"Yes," she said.

He released her, pulled her into the lounge, and closed the sliding door.

"I want to bend you over my couch soon," he said as he scooped her into his arms like she weighed nothing then strode down the passage.

It was strange to be carried. Looping her arms around his neck, she held on. She feathered kisses across any part of him she could reach, twisting to lick his nipple. He growled, his shoulders shuddering.

Alongside his bed, he lowered her feet to the floor and peeled her onesie down, trapping her arms. He grabbed the lowered onesie collar and crushed her against him, claiming her mouth. The taste of him seared into her memory. He nibbled along her jaw to her earlobe, and she clutched his waist. In time too, because her knees buckled.

He yanked her onesie until it gathered on her calves, and with a push, she fell onto the bed, bouncing on her back. Her pink onesie went flying, but she didn't have time to comment. He grasped her ankles, spreading her legs when he trailed his hands down to her inner thighs. When he leaned over her, the bulge in his yoga pants pressed at her entrance. He kissed her, one arm holding his weight off her as he teased her nipple with the other hand. She ran her nails along his shoulder and down his bicep, clinging and clawing his back. She kissed him, dueling with his tongue for supremacy and gladly losing.

He dusted kisses down her neck, nibbling near her collarbone before claiming a pert nipple. She breathed his name, chanting it as she pleaded for mercy she didn't want. He feathered kisses over her stomach, twirling the tip of his tongue around her belly button. With his path clear, she jerked, tugging on his shoulders to dissuade him.

She cried out at his touch, at his tongue, and writhed beneath his onslaught. When he sucked on her, she screamed, splintering under an exquisite explosion of sensations sending shivers through her and hardening her nipples. Arching her back and shuddering, she buried her fingers in his cool hair. He lunged back, peeled off his yoga pants, then climbed onto the bed, hiking her legs as he rubbed the tip of his cock where she pulsed with pleasure.

The feel of him stretching her, his trembling arms as he held himself above her had her leaning up to claim his mouth, tasting herself on his tongue. No matter how she begged him, he kept a smooth, relaxed rhythm. She needed him to dominate her, to thrust her off the edge teasing at her senses.

Moaning, she raised her pelvis by tightening her legs around his hips, urging him on. He didn't budge, just slid in and out, peppering her with kisses while burying his fingers in her hair. With each stroke, he hit her G-spot, triggering wave after wave of pleasure until she lost count. The slightest tilt of his plunge had her orgasming again.

"Tessa." With a groan, he thrust into her, slamming her back. He claimed her mouth for a kiss as his body shuddered against her. "So good," he whispered against her lips.

Still inside her, he fell to the side, taking her with him. Sprawled across his body, with his chest heaving and a fine sheen of sweat coating them, she stroked his skin, trying to catch her breath. If she didn't know better, she'd call this lovemaking. His caresses and slow strokes pulled on her heartstrings and had her analyzing every expression crossing his face. There was safety in good, hard sex. It satiated her body but had no impact on emotions.

Could she survive five more days? Would she end up losing her heart in London to a mafia boss with killer blue eyes? She kissed his shoulder and allowed him to tug her flush against him. She was an old hat at broken hearts. If he did break hers, then she'd heal, eventually. What else could she do?

Chapter Fourteen

Awaking without an alarm as a man feathered gentle kisses along her bare shoulder must be two of the best ways to greet the day. Tessa moaned, snuggled into his embrace, and tightened his arm around her waist.

"I thought you'd never wake up," Cam said in that rasp of his that promised so much more than just sinful nights. There was something intense in his voice she wished she could bottle.

"You should've tried harder." She arched her back for a stretch.

"If you keep rubbing your backside against me, I won't have to try at all." He nipped her shoulder then kissed the spot as if to apologize.

"I've never heard I'm a disagreeable person, tending to complain about all manner of abuse." She twisted in his arms to kiss him.

"Abuse?" he asked, between kisses of his own.

"I know your goal is to tie me to this bed, but I have a meeting with another publisher today. I'd like to walk like a lady. At this point, I'll sashay like a satisfied hooker." She kissed his throat, then nipped his shoulder in payback.

"Tie you to the bed?" He laughed, his chest shaking with it. "I'd love that."

"Yup, and something to do with a leather couch. Time is ticking, Mr. Mathews, and I'm not a patient woman."

"You are, and I love that about you. Wanna go for breakfast? And eat?" The hope in his eyes had her admitting her lifestyle could take a backseat until she went home.

"I'd love to eat bacon with you." Then she squealed when he rolled her over and under him.

"Right answer, Tessa-luv." He snatched deep kisses from her until she was breathless with desire.

"I'm just a girl, lying beneath a boy, hoping he'd offer her bacon." She ran her fingertips over his ribs.

"There's that sass," he said. "I'd like to think it's me who swayed you, but according to my extensive research, it's the bacon."

She stared into his smoky-blue eyes and shook her head. "I can have bacon any day. I can't have Camden Mathews. So, if you want to spend the day cleaning hair out of shower drains, I'm your girl."

His mood turned somber, leaving her to wonder if she'd said something wrong. He pressed an urgent kiss to her lips, the humor in his eyes replaced with that now-familiar intensity she prayed wasn't contagious. This was a fling, a short affair in London with a man she could never keep.

"Right answer," he said, his raspy voice more potent. He cradled her face in his hands and sipped from her lips. Gone was the fierce passion, replaced with this gentler side of him. It made her feel cherished despite a shiver of fear settling in her chest.

"So, bacon or shower drains? I've got to dress for the occasion." She tried to lighten the mood before tears swept her away. They clawed at the back of her throat and burned behind her eyes. She'd lose it when she was on the flight. No way would she waste a moment with him by crying.

"Bacon," he said.

"Bike or car?" She spread her thighs so that he nestled where her sex thrummed.

He groaned, snatching another kiss from her even as she looped her legs around his hips. "It'll be the bed if you keep this up. I do believe you're seducing me, sweetheart."

"I am not." She chuckled. "If I was, I'd gyrate."

"You'd what?" He pushed off her to meet her gaze.

She demonstrated a twirl of her hips, brushing his morning arousal.

He sucked in a breath. "Temptress."

Grabbing her hands, he held them above her head. He gathered her wrists in one hand and dropped his other to her breast, pinching her nipple. Her gyration this time had nothing to do with seduction and more to do with need. His touch traveled lower, and within minutes, she saw stars and white heat, leaving her with delightful tingles rippling down her spine.

He pulled away, and she scowled, wondering why he wasn't finding his pleasure. She *had* said something wrong. Shame was swift to strike, and as she watched his sculpted backside disappear into the bathroom, she curled into a ball. Tears pressed at her, demanding release. What a fool she was to read his intense expressions as something more. He was probably constipated. She smothered a manic giggle, hating how dirty she felt as if she'd sold herself for nothing more than free room and board.

Gathering her things, she showered in the guest bathroom. She scrubbed herself over and over in the hopes it would wash away the heartache. Just sex with no strings attached. She was a grown woman; she could do this. If only he was consistent. If he treated her like a lover, she could act like one. Her fault was in relaxing her guard. The formidable man she'd met at *Elysium* was still there, and she needed to remember that.

Oh, how she hated emotional turmoil or drama of any sort. She sure as hell wasn't going to be at the center of a meltdown. Sucking in calming breaths, she yanked on her black military-style leggings and off-the-shoulder baggy camo-green shirt. Socks and boots followed before she was out the door and heading to his room to finish dressing.

"I was hoping you'd join me." He tugged on a white T-shirt that hugged every hard edge of his torso.

"I thought you wanted a little privacy." She dropped her chin to her chest to hide her despair.

With a fingertip under her chin, he raised her mouth for a quick kiss. Damn him for confusing her. "You said you wanted to walk straight." His slow smile formed a dimple in one cheek.

"I'm good at other things too." She groaned, disbelieving she pimped herself like that to Cam. "I'm sorry. I'm not a desperate and horny housewife, I promise." Had she not just moments ago berated herself for her slutty behavior? This wasn't a movie where she had a chance to snag the rich guy.

He chuckled, crushing her against him for a hug. "You can show me later."

"I can't believe you chose bacon over me," she teased with a fake gasp. "I'm mortified." She pulled out of his arms to run a brush through her hair. "You didn't say, so I dressed for the bike." While braiding her hair, she studied the contents of her luggage, searching for her cosmetics bag. Bathroom? "Almost done, give me two minutes."

"That's what all women say," he said, lacing his black boots.

She smirked at him and re-joined him two minutes later. Eyeliner, mascara, and perfume didn't take long. "Ready." She strode past him with a triumphant grin.

Brunch was at a lovely café outside MacMurray Publishing's building. They laughed like vacationers with every topic open for discussion except the elephant in the room—her departure. When the time for her appointment came, she kissed his lips and crossed the street, entering the two-story building through their wooden double doors.

The meeting was swift and devastating. Her mind reeled, replaying each negative word as she relived the rejection. Her earlier joy shattered. When she stepped out into overcast skies, a self-mocking smile twitched at her lips. Her fantasy novel was too similar to one they had on their lists, and her heart echoed the solemnity of the weather. It was almost one in the afternoon; people scurried about their business despite the threatening thunder clouds. Drawing a shuddering breath, she chastised herself for the sadness dampening her spirits. As a writer, rejections were par for the course, but a face-to-face meant having to hold herself together in the presence of others.

Sharpening her gaze, she spotted Cam—his brow furrowed. That he waited for her was a needed reminder life went on. Perhaps this publisher wouldn't have been a good fit? At least they'd given her feedback instead of the automated rejection email. She strode toward the Mugs McGee café, dodging the lunch crowd using the courtyard even though the weather had turned sour.

When she paused in her stride to capture a stray ray of sunlight, someone jabbed a hard object into her back. A glance over her shoulder revealed many details. Logan's goon from last night? The gun barrel at her right shoulder was good, showing that he'd come alone, and he was close, no doubt to hide his actions. Perhaps panic should've sunk in, but she didn't have the emotional capacity to deal with this today.

"Is this necessary?" She spread her legs into an active stance and raised her right hand to rest on her collarbone.

"Mr. Logan requires your company," the man said, digging the gun into her shoulder blade.

"Sore about last night?" she asked, unable to resist prodding the bear. "Did little old me hurt you?"

He grunted, and as he did so, she twisted her right shoulder forward, spun to the left, and wrapped her arm over his wrist. She tightened her hold, squeezing his arm between her chest and armpit. He jerked, but she held firm, slapping her other hand over the slide of his gun, and pushed it away.

Sweat formed on her brow; he was a big bastard, but she was glad he had a gun. Those were easier to disarm. When he struggled, she held on, hurrying through the next steps. A knee to the groin had him dropping forward with a groan, then she twisted the weapon from his fingers, almost breaking his thumb before guiding it out of his grip. She emptied the clip and slipped the bullets into her pocket.

"That's it, Logan." She faced a hovering shadow, tossed the pistol at him, and gestured with her head to the café. "Let's resolve this now."

"I don't ..." Logan paused, casting a scowl at his goon.

"Do you think I give a shit what you think? If you want *Elysium*, you'll come with me. Now." Her voice stuttered as adrenaline drained from her. She strolled to where Cam waited, having just burst through the door. Hugging herself, she hoped no one could see her trembling knees.

Dealing with a rubber gun at Krav Maga was a far cry to the real thing. Something she'd keep in mind when she returned to class.

Chapter Fifteen

CAM YANKED HER INTO his arms, kissing her forehead. It felt too good being there. For that reason alone—her need for comfort—she left his embrace and entered the café. An almond milk cappuccino awaited her, and she sank into her seat with gratitude, cupping the hot mug like a lifeline.

Many things could have gone wrong. The gun could have discharged as she twisted away from it. She could've shot someone when she'd shoved it to the side. The goon could've used his bulk better, and she had to leap up to knee him in the groin due to the height difference between them. Shit, he could've drawn another weapon. She didn't doubt he had more on his person.

Cam stole a chair from another table to sit next to her. Logan dropped into the one opposite them. They stared at each other in sullen silence. She ignored them, taking a much-needed sip of her coffee.

"How long have you known each other?" she asked, allowing a deep sigh to escape her. Sensei had never mentioned the drop in energy after a life-threatening situation. Her body was languid to the tips of her toes. A nap would've been nice about now.

"Since teenagers," Cam said.

"Right, and when did you make this deal? To improve the way you do business?"

"The first year we met," Logan said before ordering an espresso.

She almost giggled but couldn't be bothered. Strong, black, and bitter; yes, his choice suited him. "And the deal stands? Or have you changed your mind?" She met Logan's gray eyes. He was a gorgeous man; it was a pity bitterness tugged his lips into a perpetual frown.

"It stands," he said, an octave above a whisper.

"Okay, so *Elysium* and Gina are the reasons for all this?" She raised a finger and circled it.

Logan nodded.

Cam placed a hand on her knee and left it there. The act was intimate, sensual, and comforting.

She needed the latter more. "Gina's resolved?"

"In a way." Logan lifted the dainty espresso cup to his lips.

"Did you apologize to Cam?" she asked, too tired to care if her questions were offensive.

"No," Cam said. His gruff voice revealed his anger, his bouncing knee his frustration, and the downward pull of his sensual lips his sadness.

"So, not resolved. Well, regarding *Elysium*, will you adhere to my decision or ignore it?"

"I'll stand by whatever you decide." Cam squeezed her knee.

She wanted to rail at these men. How dare they place this on her shoulders? They did need a somewhat-neutral arbitrator, but bloody hell, why did it have to be her? She shot a glare at them both. Logan endangering her every damn day had forced her hand. Cam was too frustrated to think of an alternative solution.

"Yes, I'll stand by it." Logan's agreement surprised her. Had he not believed Cam when he'd said she'd decide? Judging by his goon-plus-gun episode, no, yet here he sat, agreeing. How duplicitous was this man?

"Good. You'll share in *Elysium*, fifty-fifty." *Done.* She released her breath, downed the coffee, and rose, scraping her chair back. Cam did too, concern marring his handsome features. "I'll send Anthony back. You two iron out the details, and I'll see you when you get home." She kissed his cheek and left the café.

The moment she stepped onto the dreary sidewalk, long fingers wrapped around her throat, lifted her off the ground, and slammed her against the brick wall. Her back throbbed a greeting. Logan's goon had her pinned, and with his meaty hand, she couldn't break his hold. Pain lanced up her throat, and stars burst across her vision as she struggled to breathe. Sensei had said she'd have seconds to react.

Panic gripped her, swift and sharp, crushing her chest and narrowing her focus. She stretched forward to embed her thumbs in his eyes. He jerked back, out of reach. So, she pressed her heels to the wall and pushed off it. He didn't budge, just squeezed harder. Black circled her vision, and her lungs burned, crying out for air.

Her children crossed her mind, and as a tear ran over her cheek, she bid them a silent farewell.

He fell backward, releasing her, and she slid down the wall, landing on her knees. She racked in agonizing breaths, coughing as she did so. The air was sweet, the cold breeze refreshing on her flushed face. Cam scooped her into his arms and rushed her to the car, where Anthony held the door open. He placed her on the seat, then climbed in on the other side.

"Tessa, how are you feeling? I'm so sorry. I shouldn't have let you leave. I didn't want you to go." He tugged her into his arms, crushing her against him, babbling words as he stroked her hair with trembling fingers. "I'm taking you to the hospital."

She opened her mouth to speak, but the pain was too much, like there was glass shards in her throat. Whimpering, she buried her fingers into his chest. Her tears ran free at her inability to speak and at the agony lacerating her. She blamed shock for turning her into a blubbering mess.

The trip was quick. He carried her through the automated doors. She wanted to tell him there was nothing wrong with her legs and slapping his hands away had no effect. With a sigh, she looped her arms around his neck and nuzzled his T-shirt.

"I'm fine," she rasped, forcing the words out. They sounded like shredding paper, and she gave up. The fire grating her throat was too excruciating to bother trying again.

He shushed her too. "Don't speak."

A nurse escorted them to a bed where Cam draped her onto it. She sat upright but sank back into the pillow. A young doctor smiled a quick greeting, stroked, and prodded her throat, using her moans as feedback.

"We must do a few x-rays, an MRI, if need be. I'm afraid it's overnight for you," he said. She groaned, at the expense, at the waste of time. All of this was inconvenient, and she abhorred that. "Mr. Mathews, please go with Nurse Elaine to fill in the paperwork."

Cam nodded, kissed Tessa's forehead, and left the room.

"Your name?" the doctor asked. He held out his notepad for her to write on. She did so. "Tessa, I'm Dr. Leibowitz. Tell me, did Mr. Mathews abuse you?"

She shook her head then whimpered when pain lanced up her neck; the bruised muscles protesting any sharp movement. She scrawled on the pad a brief synopsis of what had happened.

"Good. Any trouble breathing? No. Did you lose consciousness? How were you strangled? Two hands?" As he questioned her, she answered on the pad. "And lastly, did you think you were going to die?"

She gasped, the faces of her children coming to mind. A tear streaked down her cheek. Fiddling with the collar of the gown, she managed a tight nod.

"Well, let's hope there are no long-lasting effects. You'll be fine, Tessa. I'd be remiss in my duties if I didn't mention months, years from now, this places you at risk of carotid dissection, pulmonary edema, hemorrhagic and ischemic stroke."

At his medical terms, she blinked. She'd need to research those before she let it worry her.

"Thank you," she rasped, then smiled when Cam hurried into the room.

Dr. Leibowitz gave her something for the pain, and she dozed between x-rays and MRI scans. After all the tests, they wheeled her into a private ward. She arched a brow at Cam at the expenditure, but she couldn't berate him for it. As long as she didn't have to pay; she would've had to sell her house. He didn't go, despite her nudging her head at the door. No nurse ushered him out when visiting hours had passed.

"I'm not leaving you." He leaned over the bed to grab her hand. "It's my fault this happened to you, Tessa. I'm so sorry."

She shook her head, but he wouldn't listen to her. Regret, despair, and anger twisted his face. "My fault," she said, keeping her voice soft. She'd pushed that goon to this point, hadn't been vigilant, and had assumed Logan had better control over his men.

"No, don't ever think that." Cam pressed a gentle kiss to her knuckles.

"Logan's?" she said and chuckled, wincing when her throat complained despite the medication.

The doctor came in with the test results. That the damage was minimal delighted him. Something about the firm grasp not allowing her to put up a fight and cause hemorrhaging. If he only knew how hard she'd fought, but her efforts had been like a rag doll clutched in a toddler's merciless grip.

"I'm still keeping you overnight. Let me know if you struggle to breathe or swallow. I'll schedule a laryngoscopy in the morning."

She smiled, pointed at the doctor's notepad, and he left it with her. She scrawled a note to Cam, telling him to go home and rest.

"I'm staying," he said, a pulse ticking at the base of his clenched jaw.

Writing another note, she handed the pad to him and scooted up. She didn't have to ask him twice. He toed off his shoes and crawled in with her, pulling her against him. With featherlight kisses across her forehead and the pain medication taking effect, he lulled her to sleep.

Chapter Sixteen

CAM WAS LIVID. THERE was no other way to explain the fury stiffening his muscles as he relived seeing Patrick pin Tessa against the wall. At that moment, he had stopped breathing, his heart in his throat with fear paralyzing him. Logan and Anthony had reacted first, yanking Patrick away from her. She'd fallen to the paving, sucking in breaths with tears rolling down her cheeks.

He'd never seen her so vulnerable.

Rage had torn through him then, and he'd taken a step toward Patrick, murder in mind. Logan had commanded him to see to Tessa. She needed urgent care. Shame had been swift to strike Cam. She should've been his priority.

Lying next to her in the hospital bed and inhaling her tantalizing fragrance, he cherished holding her in his arms. He could've lost her today. The pain that cinched his chest when he thought of her leaving was nothing compared to the crushing weight constricting his breathing. He had to let her go.

Having her in his life meant certain death for her, and despite the emotions she invoked within him, none of it mattered. She deserved to live a good life. This meant one away from him. Sorrow settled in the depths of his soul, and his eyes stung with unshed tears. Blinking at the water droplet on her shoulder, he frowned, having not shed a tear since his father's death.

He'd loved Tessa from the moment she thanked him for a kiss. Acknowledging this didn't ease the agony knowing he'd never see her again. He dipped his head and brushed a kiss over her parted lips. The white bandages wrapped around her neck reminded him of her suffering.

It would've been safer for her had he not pursued her. Regret was a harsh emotion, highlighting his selfish behavior. He wanted her to blame him, but she hadn't. Despite the pain she was in, she managed to smile and tease him. The bright addictive warmth of love flooded his chest, and he crushed her against him, needing to capture this moment.

He assumed Logan would deal with Patrick. He'd better, or he'd have to deal with Cam. Tessa's decision regarding *Elysium* had been strategic. Knowing how her mind worked, forcing them to co-own the club meant healing their friendship.

Her departure loomed like roiling thunderclouds, dampening the elation being with her summoned within him. He'd need to up his game and pack these last days full of adventure, creating enough memories to sustain him. A bike ride, a visit to the jewelers, a romantic dinner followed by dancing.

He replayed the afternoon and remembered her sadness after leaving the publishers. She hadn't received an offer for her book. He could buy out MacMurray Publishing and rescind the rejection. If she found out, she'd be furious, but what could she do, fly back to chastise him? He chuckled, imagining her doing just that.

How he loved her.

"How is she?" Logan asked, keeping his voice low.

Cam twitched, having not heard his friend enter. "The doctor thinks she'll make a full recovery," he said. "Patrick?" His throat seized, and he struggled to speak past the man's name. His body trembled, and a soft moan from Tessa tightened his hold on her, letting her ground him.

"Reassigned." Logan dropped into a nearby chair and rested his elbows on his knees. "I haven't killed anyone since Dad died. I'm not about to start now."

"As long as Tessa's safe, then I'll accept your decision. But I want a man on him, in case he goes rogue." Cam maintained eye contact, watching for any inflection crossing Logan's features. He was being overly cautious; he had a right to be.

"Done. I'll talk to Marc about *Elysium*. You stay and take care of your woman."

"She's not mine," Cam said but didn't manage to keep the sorrow from his voice.

"The way you're holding her says otherwise." Logan knew him too well, earning a grunt from Cam. "Sorry about this. It was...unexpected." He grimaced, running a hand over his face. "Sorry about Gina, too. I should've known you wouldn't touch her."

"I forgive you, as always." Cam shared a boyish smile that was reminiscent of their childhood. "What did she say when you confronted her?"

"That she was old, single, and wanted children. Something about you showing promise and other excuses she could think of." Logan chuckled, but it rang with sadness. "What a fool I was, Cam. My sister pulling a stunt like this." He rose to his full height before grinning, his youthful mischief sneaking in. "I carted her off to our country estate. Under serious guard, so she can't leave, shop online, or cause any trouble."

Cam chuckled. Gina would hate that. His mirth dwindled at the realization that she had jeopardized their friendship. She used to be the only woman he could speak to without judgment. Now, that woman was Tessa, asleep in his arms and trusting him to care for her. He kissed her hospital-gowned shoulder.

"I see why you love her," Logan said, drawing a scowl from Cam. Did everyone know how he felt? "You know you can't keep her, right?"

Cam narrowed his eyes at Logan, conveying how much he hated the reminder. "Yes."

"You'd have to give up your life of crime if you want her."

"Logan," Cam hissed. "I don't need a bloody lecture."

"Fine, I'll leave you to it. I'll send flowers in the morning."

"Flowers?" Cam arched a brow. Logan wasn't sentimental or considerate.

"She once said I should send flowers if I wanted to thank her. I think the same is true for apologies." Logan circled the bed and rested his hand on Cam's shoulder. "I'll send many bouquets. She'll know what they mean. Goodnight, Cam."

Cam nodded, his thoughts replaying Logan's words. Give up a life of crime to keep her? He let his mind toy with the idea. How he could end all this; liquidate his assets, set up a trust fund for Selena, and move to Africa. The magnitude of such a task was daunting and impossible. His enemies would follow him.

Minutes after Logan left, a nurse hurried in to take Tessa's blood pressure and temperature. She didn't say anything upon finding Cam in the bed. When she left, he did overhear her conversation with a fellow nurse about how he'd spoil his fiancé with such care.

Fiancé? He sucked in a sharp breath. Hope struck a swift blow made more devastating when he had to deflate it. The tear that slipped out was beyond his control, and in the quiet of the hospital room, he mourned.

Chapter Seventeen

When Tessa awoke, it was to an empty bed and room. The weight of Cam's arm didn't pin her to the bed, and the loss of it skewered her heart with sadness. She drew in a careful breath, forcing back the tears. There had to be a silver lining, even if she couldn't see it. As she crawled from the bed, with her ass bare, she valued the privacy to do so without losing her dignity. Stroking the bandage around her throat, she padded across the cold floor to the en suite. The beeps and muted voices from the passage didn't penetrate the quiet within the room. Loneliness plagued her, but she couldn't expect Cam to wait on her hand and foot.

They'd performed the laryngoscopy first thing this morning, and she'd fallen asleep upon returning to the room.

Her time in London was ending. Determination and a backbone would force her to step onto the plane and leave Cam forever. A part of her longed for him to speak words of endearment, to beg her to stay. Another part of her wouldn't abandon her children, regardless of their age. They were old enough to stand on their own two feet, but a life without them was unimaginable.

She'd spoken to them about emigration, but they were adamant South Africa was their home. So, asking them to move to London would be met with a resounding no. Then again, she was alone now with Forest managing the divorce proceedings. Using her electronic signature, she'd signed the documents a day ago. She didn't know how long it would take to become a divorcee. Forest planned to move out before she returned. It felt final, like a chunk of her life had ended, and she was powerless to alter the events leading up to it.

Pain should have seized her chest, but only numbness nestled there. Perhaps later, she'd find the ability to care or to lament the loss of so many years. After splashing water on her face, she dried herself with a towel. When she left the bathroom, a rack of clothing not her own dominated the space.

"What the—"

"How do you feel?" Cam bounded out of the chair and crossed to her.

The sight of him elevated her heartbeat and skittered excitement along her nerve endings. He was as handsome as the day she met him, meaning the attraction had yet to fade—even a little. His damp blond hair cascaded over his forehead. His blue eyes sparkled. He clasped her hands and tugged her toward the garments.

"Good," she said, her voice husky with a sting in her throat.

"Marc chose to send these over instead of pilfering from your luggage. Sometimes, it's best not to argue with him." Cam smiled.

"Designer labels." She flipped through the hangers while admiring the exquisite items. Each one would be an asset in anyone's wardrobe.

"They're all designed with steampunk in mind. That is your style?"

She sliced a startled glance at him, impressed he knew a little about fashion. "Yes, aspects of it."

She swallowed, fighting the closing sensation in her throat. The more she spoke, the more shards of glass sliced across her throat, or so it felt. High-waisted dark-gray trousers snared her attention, and she removed them from the hanger to place them on the bed. A burgundy blouse followed.

"Accessories are in here." He set a thin, black suitcase on the bed before flipping it open.

She gave a silent gasp at the beautifully detailed belts, buckles, brooches, pocket watches, and bracelets. They looked expensive. She brushed a fingertip along a cogged bracelet, embedded with zips and leather. A gold necklace with cogs, blue gemstones, and a carved dragonfly caught her eye. She wouldn't accept any of them, not wanting Cam to pay for such an indulgence. The clothes were a necessity, but she didn't need to abuse his thoughtfulness.

She closed the case and offered him her back, a silent request to undo the ties of her hospital gown. A quick shower, donning her new clothes, then her boots, and she'd be ready to leave. He undid the ties with caressing fingers, sending shivers along her skin.

"The doctor discharged me?" She hoped to leave the hospital and her near-death experience behind her.

"Yes." He kissed her exposed shoulder. "You don't like any of the pieces?"

"They're beautiful, and it was thoughtful to include them, but you know I don't wear jewelry." She faced him, and in doing so, disrobed with the edges of the gown clasped in his hands.

His gaze traveled her body, a lustful intensity claiming his features. His breath rushed out, and his trembling fingers crushed the fabric.

"Shower before I claim you where you stand," he said, his voice hoarse.

She froze, disbelieving he'd find her attractive—unclean, disheveled, and as bruised as she was.

"Don't look at me like that, Tessa. You ooze sex appeal."

"It's my fault?" she asked in a whisper.

Explaining why she wouldn't choose from the accessories had taken the last of her speech ability. Pain scoured her with each breath but telling him about it was out of the question. He snatched a hard kiss from her, grabbed her shoulders, and nudged her toward the bathroom.

"I'll make sure you're discharged." He strode from the room.

With a sigh, she attended to her ablutions. She wasn't surprised the trousers and shirt fit as if made for her. Dressed and drying her hair with a towel, she left the bathroom. On the bedside table was a tray of steaming tea. She moaned, tossed the towel on the bed, and poured a cup. The first sip had heated bliss sliding down her throat, soothing and burned a path to her stomach.

"Good, you found the tea. Hungry?" Cam scooped up the towel to rub her hair with gentle strokes. She shook her head before taking another sip, savoring each mouthful. It was too early for food, and she couldn't imagine swallowing anything solid. "Want to do anything today?"

She looked at him over the rim of her cup, turning her body to do so. She wanted to spend the day snuggled on the couch, with him warming her side. The telly would be on, and she'd have a hot cup of soup in her hands. "You... Couch... Telly... Soup," she said. If she could find orgasmic bliss in his arms, that would be a bonus.

"Are you in pain?" He pulled a bottle out of his pocket to shake two capsules onto his palm. "The doctor prescribed these."

Drinking water to do so, she swallowed one at a time. She sat on the chair to tug her boots on and draped her dirty clothes over an arm before giving Cam a thumbs up, indicating her readiness. A nurse pushed a wheelchair in, and with a sigh, she crossed to it.

"How are you, Tess-luv?" Marc stepped into the room.

She flashed a welcoming smile when he kissed her temple. "Thanks." She plucked at her shirt to convey what she meant.

He nodded, darting a glance between her and Cam. "I'll have them deliver the remaining garments to the penthouse," he said. He dropped to his haunches alongside the wheelchair, his long fingers gripping its arm. "And don't argue, or I'll have them delivered to your South African home, instead."

"Do so anyway, Marc," Cam said.

"Just because I can't speak..." she said, sparking fresh shards of fire along her throat. They were muted with the pain meds kicking in, but still present.

The nurse spun the wheelchair with ease, and Tessa missed their responses. When she arrived home, she'd send the package back, unopened. She sensed Cam striding behind her but not close enough to talk to her. That was fine when she couldn't speak anyway.

Anthony rushed to help her, stooping to lift her out of the wheelchair. She smacked his hands away and jumped to her feet in case he tried again. Standing to the side, Cam chuckled while Anthony hurried to open the car door before she reached it. With a sigh, she climbed in and shuffled along the seat, placing her clothes between her and the other door.

Cam followed, but instead of staying on his side, he pulled her onto his lap, settling his lips on hers in one swift move. She gasped, unprepared for his onslaught. He gathered her to him, yet despite the awkward position, she wouldn't ask him to release her. Not with four days left. Every minute with him she'd cherish, and each second would be spent with no regrets.

It was a pity she'd lost her heart in London.

Chapter Eighteen

TESSA CURLED UP ON the couch in one of Cam's T-shirts, her cheek on her palm with her head in his lap. Soft noises escaped her, and he smiled. At last, something that could irritate him, but even her snoring he found adorable. He brushed hair off her temple and sighed, wishing for something he wouldn't dare consider. Stroking her bare hip was all he'd allow himself to touch. A half-empty container of chicken soup sat on the coffee table. The telly played a reality show of some sort. He'd muted it when he realized she'd fallen asleep.

Bouquets filled his apartment with heady fragrances twitching his nose. Logan had overdone it. She'd reacted with delighted gratitude until he told her who they were from. When she burst into a full-bodied laugh, the wild, carefree joy of it had filled his chest with warmth. He loved it when she laughed. She'd paid for it though, losing her voice for a good hour.

Her phone made a different noise than normal, and she jerked awake, her hand flying out to grab it. She scanned the message, her mouth gaping before she rolled onto her back to look at him.

"What's this?" She thrust her phone into his line of sight.

He focused on the email. It was from the publisher who'd rejected her. They asked if she was behind the hostile takeover. He scowled. Someone had beat him to it, and he had a sneaking suspicion he knew that person well.

"Looks like the publishing house is under new management."

"Yours?" she whispered. Fear crinkled the corners of her eyes, and his heart cracked at the pain crossing her face. For once, he was grateful he hadn't reacted on instinct. Buying out the publishers would've driven a wedge between them.

"No," he said. "I thought about doing it, but after the attack, you were my only concern."

Grinning, she rolled over onto her knees before rising to kiss his chin, nose, and each cheek. "Sex." She nipped his bottom lip.

His heart leaped into his throat, and he wrapped his arms around her, crushing her against him. "I don't want you in pain, sweetheart."

"Me, quiet," she said between brushes of her lips.

His balls twitched as she continued to tempt him with her mouth, sweeping her tongue across his bottom lip before pulling away. Unable to resist, he cupped the back of her head to hold her in place. He needed to taste her, to show her how much he wanted her.

As he plundered her mouth, she made no sound, but her fingers feathered across his face, toyed with his earlobes, and tangled in his hair. She kissed him back, pressing her pebbled breasts to his T-shirt-covered chest. He spread his thighs to cater for his erection—his jeans tightening to a painful degree.

She broke the kiss first, sucking in breaths as she tugged on his shirt. He whipped it off in time to see her do the same, her breasts bouncing free. A moan tore from him when she rubbed them against his chest; the skin-on-skin contact made him shudder. Need pooled in his groin. She threw a leg over his lap until she straddled him. Her sex spread wide across his bulge ripped a growl from him. He wanted nothing more than to strip, to grip her hips, and to thrust upward.

She must've felt the same, for she un-straddled him to undo his belt, unzip his jeans, and work her hand inside. He wriggled to loosen his jeans enough for his cock to spring free. She flashed him a delighted smile, running kisses along his jaw, down his neck to nip a nipple. At the same time, she wrapped her fingers around his length.

"You're killing me," he said, following his words with a groan when she ran her hand up and down.

Tingling pleasure traveled from his shaft and up his spine. She slipped her fingers lower to cup his balls when she flicked her tongue over the tip of his cock. head. He jerked, thrusting upward, bright bursts of joy mixed with need took over his responses.

He scowled at his reaction like he was an untried schoolboy. Everything within him wanted in her now. But if she took him in her mouth, it might hurt her. He assumed working her jaw would tax her throat muscles. Grabbing her knee, he tugged her on top of him, her wet heat coating the length of him.

"Impale yourself," he said.

"Condom," she rasped, holding out her hand.

He dug into his back pocket to hand her the packet. She tore it open with her teeth, and when she rolled it onto him, the sensations were too exquisite for words. The friction of her stroking him, sliding the condom on, then stroking him again until he was well-covered, was something a woman hadn't done for him in a long time. It was an untapped pleasurable experience.

She rose onto her knees and shuffled forward until the head of his cock pressed at her entrance. Then, with her hands gripping his shoulders, she lowered herself. He sank his fingers into her hips, holding onto her as inch by inch she guided him in. She leaned back when she was fully seated, her mouth falling open on a silent gasp. As she undulated, rubbing her channel along his cock, tingles barreled along the length of him, rushing him toward an orgasm—he was that close. Darts of excitement shot from his balls to his tip.

Wrapping an arm around her hips, he flipped her onto her back and pounded into her, unable to slow his thrusting or his enjoyment of their union. His desire for her hadn't diminished in the days spent with her. It had increased to an obsession.

"Tess." He nipped her earlobe before brushing his lips down her neck.

Sucking on her pulse there had her arching, lifting her hips to meet his downward thrust. She mewled, and heat gushed over him, catapulting him over the edge. He shuddered. Pure bliss flooded his spine, and he closed his eyes to relish it.

"Good sex," she whispered, running kisses along his collarbone to his chin.

He collapsed on top of her, only now acknowledging the burn on his back from where she'd embedded her short nails. At some point, she'd wrapped her legs around his hips and had yet to release him. He wouldn't complain, although, still wearing his jeans was tactless of him. Bloody hell, she drove him so insane with desire he forgot everything but the feel and taste of her.

"You're addictive," he said, claiming her mouth for another kiss. He prayed the taste of her infused his cells and saturated his mind so when he yearned for her, this part of her remained with him.

"Ditto," she said in a breathless moan as he placed wet kisses down her collarbone.

His phone chimed, and he scowled at the offending device. A sigh tore from him. He pressed his temple to hers, fighting for patience, then pushed away and pulled out of her.

She arched a brow in concern, her fingers trailing his arms when he stepped out of reach.

"My sister is on her way up."

"What?" She mouthed the question, swinging her legs off the couch to hop up, yanking on his shirt in the process.

Her sexy ass disappearing exploded fury through his veins. The dark weight crushing his chest was dread. How long had he half-lived? How long had he sacrificed enjoyment for obligation? What did Selena want now?

"Shower." She nudged him toward his room.

He had no intention of showering alone, but he did disappear into the bathroom to dispose of the condom. Zipping his jeans, he returned to find Tessa making a cup of tea. His front door opened, and Selena waltzed in, her disheveled clothing indicative of a wild night out.

"Marc said you were home." She climbed onto the barstool, the stench of smoke and alcohol assaulting his nostrils. "I assumed you were alone."

"Hello to you too." Taking a bottle of water out of the fridge, he uncapped it and took a long draw. "This is Tessa, Selena. I assume you're planning on spending the night? I'd rather call Anthony to take you home."

"I can see why." She glared at Tessa, her lips twisting with distaste as she ran her judgmental gaze over his woman.

The urge to slap her had him gripping his bottle until the plastic crackled under the force. Tessa lowered her gaze, and when she raised it, humor crinkled her brown eyes. He released his pent-up breath.

Unfazed, she waved hello, flashing a sweet smile before sipping her tea. He marveled at how sensual she looked in his T-shirt, her muscled legs crossed at the ankles, and her hair in wild disarray. He'd done that to her hair and kiss-swollen lips.

"Earth to Cam. I can't go home. Mom's there." Selena's pout didn't look good on a woman of her age.

"I'll pay for a hotel room," he said, desperate not to waste the last few days he had with Tessa. His sister was a handful, requiring way too much attention.

"Cam," Tessa said, shaking her head.

He leaned his ass against the counter beside her and curled her body into his. Caving in to the temptation to kiss her temple, he threw an arm around her and gathered her closer.

"As long as you can be quiet," she whispered. Her brown eyes sparkled with mischief, and he chuckled.

He hardened at the imagery playing through his mind, burying himself in her in the silent hours of the night. "Fine, Selena, but one night only. Tomorrow you'll check into a hotel of your choice." He arched a brow at Tessa, implying he would negotiate no further. "Pain pills and bed for you, Tessa-luv." He bounded to the lounge to fetch her medication. The quicker she finished her tea, the quicker she'd be in bed, filling his arms.

"Is this the bitch who ruined Gina's plans?"

He stilled, his head shooting up as the roar of rage deafened his thoughts and canceled his restraint. "What do you know about this miscarriage nonsense?" His voice was soft, fury driving him to focus on Selena's face, the pallor of her skin, her pupils, and the pulse ticking at her jaw. "Selena?"

She hesitated, fluffing her blonde hair while she searched for an answer. Her eyes narrowed into a calculating expression, the wheels turning in her mind. Had she and Gina created this stupid plan to entrap him? His own sister?

"Get out," he said, tapping two capsules into Tessa's cupped palm. He twisted the lid closed and placed the bottle on the counter, careful not to slam it down. When Selena hadn't moved, he tipped her stool, sending her flying. He snatched her key off the counter and tossed it into the bowl, ignoring her indignant spluttering. "I revoke your access. Return to Mom; you deserve her."

"Cam, wait, let me explain," she pleaded, but gone was the brotherly affection he'd once held for her. Bit by bit, she'd eroded it until nothing but duty remained.

"Explain what? Your scheming, your spending sprees, your promiscuity with my friends, and now this, almost costing me my friendship with Logan. I'm done. We're done." He yanked the door open and thrust her out, tossing her handbag at her before slamming the door in her face. He splayed his hands on the cool, wooden surface, sucking in sharp breaths. On the other side, she stomped and screamed. When that didn't work, she whined and pleaded. It had been adorable when she was six, but at thirty-six? No.

"Cam, please, at least call Anthony for me." The request was pitiful, but he wasn't affected.

"I'll call security," he said and chuckled when she marched down the passage.

The ever-present weight on his chest lifted. He felt freer than he had in a long while. Aware Tessa had watched his family drama play out, he squared his shoulders, preparing to meet her disgust or disapproval. Instead, she stood alongside him with her hand raised an inch from his shoulder, about to offer comfort. Concern and understanding settled on her face. He drew her into his arms and buried his nose in her hair. She hugged him back, her presence meaning more to him than any platitude she could utter.

"Cam, okay?"

"I've never been better. I'm sorry she called you a bitch."

She shrugged, her caressing fingers soothing the remnants of his anger. "Bed?"

"With you, hell, yes." He scooped her into his arms, loving her huffs of laughter.

Chapter Nineteen

TESSA STRUGGLED TO KEEP the tears at bay while she packed her bags. The last few days had been the best of her life. They'd gone on bike runs, an indoor picnic, and romantic dinners with Cam showering his full attention on her. She'd never felt this cherished. Spoiled, was what she was. As the departure date neared, sex had turned into lovemaking, and sadness had filled the lulls in their conversations.

He waited in the lounge, planning to escort her to the airport. She couldn't survive the trip *and* keep her sorrow hidden, but he'd insisted. Pasting a smile on her face was taking all her focus. Pretending excitement drained her. Drawing in a shuddering breath, she gathered her things and cast a last lingering glance across their room.

Pain squeezed her chest, stuttering her breathing and closing her throat as tears burned behind her eyes. Just another hour or two, then she could break down on the plane. Wheeling her luggage along the passage, she forced herself to take long deep breaths.

He stepped into sight, a small smile on his lips. "Ready?"

She nodded, letting him grab the handle from her. With her laptop bag slung over her shoulder, she followed him out of his apartment. The silence and tension thickened between them, worsened by the clack-clack of her luggage wheels.

"Anthony can drop me off." Her voice was too timid, but he'd been furious with her when she'd suggested he bid her farewell here instead of seeing her off.

He pressed the elevator button. "Every minute you're in London is mine. No matter how painful." Lacing his fingers through hers, he raised her hand to kiss her knuckles.

She pinched her lips and leaned into his warmth, hoping to draw strength from him.

He nuzzled her hair. "You have everything?"

"I hope so." She forced a shrug. "If not, then it wasn't important."

"Dennis said he sent through the final contract. You're clear to sign it. I'm sure Fiona's eager for you to start."

"Thank you." She climbed into the car.

As Anthony packed her things into the trunk, Cam slid in beside her. He gathered her onto his lap, his arms too tight, but she wouldn't complain.

"I'm going to miss you." He buried his nose in the curve of her neck, feathering kisses down to her collarbone then up to her jaw.

"I'll miss you too." She snuggled deeper into his embrace. Silence settled between them, and she didn't dare look out of the window to bid the glittering skyline of London farewell—too afraid it might break the dam wall.

Sooner than expected, Anthony parked in the drop-off zone. He hopped out, darting to the trunk to remove her luggage. Cam didn't move, so she didn't either, preferring to draw his cologne deep into her lungs, instead.

With a sigh, she forced her arms to release him, and as she shifted off his lap, his fingers dug into her hips for a second.

"You'll let me know when you arrive?" He cupped her cheeks with his hands, pinning her gaze to his.

She paused before she nodded. He captured her mouth for a sweet, lingering kiss that tugged on her heartstrings and weakened the dam holding her tears back. Breaking the kiss, she scrambled out of the car, sucked in the cool night air, then forced a smile for Anthony, who waited with her luggage.

"Thank you." She slipped her laptop bag over her shoulder and wrapped her fingers around her luggage handle.

Cam overlapped her hand and pulled the handle free. His jaw clenched, an indication of his determination. She led the way, striding into the airport like she knew where to go. She didn't, but he did, squeezing her elbow when he brushed past her. Drawing in a silent, shuddering breath, she trailed him, dodging fellow travelers scurrying to and from their boarding gates.

The snaking, shuffling queue to the international security checkpoint represented the end of her journey and her time with Cam. Something squeezed her chest in a vise grip, and she stumbled to a halt. He didn't notice her lagging and strode on, skipping the long queue to stand in front of the first-class counter.

She gasped and hurried across the floor, stopping beside him. He flashed his charming smile, handed over her boarding pass and passport, then wrapped an arm around her waist as he waited. She was sure she'd stowed her travel documents in her laptop bag, yet he had them. The attendant gestured to her to lay her luggage on the scale, and she did.

Watching the woman tag her bag and send it on a conveyor belt, Tessa blinked. Cam ushered her to the security checkpoint with no queue. She frowned at shuffling people and dipped her head to hide from a few glares. He squeezed her elbow. Jolting out of her daze, she plastered on a smile and placed her laptop bag on the scanner. She stared at it until it disappeared through the rubber flaps, her empty hands twitching.

This was it, the goodbye she'd dreaded. He couldn't go past this point. A tear slipped out, and she raised her face to the airport's ceiling, fighting the burgeoning emotions rising like an orchestral crescendo.

"Tess, my sweet Tess." He tugged her into his arms for a final hug.

She clung to him like a drowning swimmer. Too soon, he set her free and nudged her to the scanner. She inched toward it, and after she stepped through, she faced him, hoping to memorize this moment. Cam in his dark denims, a buttoned-up white shirt, a dark gray blazer, and his gorgeous Adonis looks.

"Bye," she mouthed, unable to project her voice with her tears squeezing her throat.

"I'm waiting for your text."

She nodded, then clutched her laptop bag in the hopes its familiar weight could stem her tears. With another deep breath, she clutched her boarding pass and passport and merged with the crowds heading to the boarding gates.

One backward glance revealed him gone, a mirage amid the darting people. He was there, then he wasn't. Air rushed out of her lungs on a moan, and something sharp twisted her gut. She struggled to breathe, to stop another tear, then another until her vision blurred, and she blindly followed on the heels of the person in front of her.

When they veered off, she raised her head, wiped her ceaseless tears to scan the boards for her departure gate. There was still time until boarding, perhaps a coffee? She found a solitary table at the closest coffee shop, and her weak knees dropped her into the chair.

The waitress placed a stack of paper towels on the table along with her almond milk cappuccino. Tessa flashed a watery smile, grabbing the towels to dab her eyes and cheeks.

She savored the coffee while tossing lingering glances at the chocolate cake on display. It wouldn't do her any good with her lactose intolerance, not when the flight was eleven hours long.

She sighed and dug in her laptop bag for her journal, needing to distract her mind. Her fingers closed around another boarding pass. She gasped. On the table sat two passes. One was the original she'd packed into her laptop bag, and the first-class one Cam gave her.

She chuckled, but it caught on a hiccup. The sneaky bastard. He'd known she wouldn't have allowed it. Spending eleven hours inconveniencing only a few people around her with her smothered sobs and sniffling was too tempting for her to reject his last gift.

The waitress, flight attendants, and passengers shared compassionate glances and touches as she boarded. Only one chair was next to hers, and it remained empty. She didn't doubt it was Cam's doing as well.

A shuddering sob tore through her when she buckled in, and as the tears streamed, her heart wailed. She loved him with every breath in her body.

But he hadn't once suggested she extend her visit or stay with him. She didn't know what hurt more, leaving him or that he didn't love her.

Chapter Twenty

Cam awoke on a bellow, sweat drenching his body.

I'm home.

Tessa's text reverberated in his mind, as it did every night. Fuck, he missed her, and no amount of time had diminished the agony squeezing his chest. He couldn't focus on work, on business dealings, and he'd lost his temper on far too many occasions.

He crawled out of bed and showered, planning on heading to the club to check in with Marc. Washing as fast as he could, he hoped to dodge memories of Tessa in the shower, beneath him, standing there at the airport with pain marring her features. Grimacing, he pulled jeans on over his damp legs, imagining Marc's expression when he strode into his office.

He wasn't welcome anywhere. Selena had stopped calling him. He wasn't going to budge on her exile. Even his mother had given up on trying to convince him to relent.

He climbed into the car, ignoring the twinge of guilt spiking amid the pain crushing his chest as if an unbearable weight rested there. Summoning Anthony at any hour was part of the job description. Still, Tessa would've frowned at what she'd consider rudeness. Anthony said nothing, nor did he show exhaustion or irritation. His suit was crisp, and his movements energetic.

Cam didn't speak either, preferring to sit in the last spot Tessa had. He sniffed the seatbelt and sighed, the tension easing from his body. Hayley had cleaned his home while he was at the airport. By the time he returned, she'd eradicated any evidence of Tessa's presence. Not even her perfume lingered in the air.

"Mr. Mathews?"

Cam jerked and raised his gaze to Anthony, who held open the door for him. Lost in his thoughts, he hadn't realized they'd arrived at *Elysium*. He slid across the seat and climbed out, bowing his in thanks.

Inside the closed club, a few employees scurried around, easing their workload for the following night. Their bustling was reminiscent of the first night he'd brought Tessa here.

Marc was behind the desk, and when Cam strode in, he tossed a glare at him. "I was just shutting down. Go home."

Cam dropped onto the couch where he'd kissed her, made love to her, slept with her in his arms. "Can't sleep."

"Or eat, or work, or do anything worthwhile. Hell, you have Logan worried, and that bloody bastard usually doesn't give a shit." Marc darted around the desk and sat on the coffee table before Cam. "Listen, Cam, it's been three fucking weeks."

Cam's shoulders slumped. Weeks? It felt like days, months, years...forever. "How do I fix this?"

Marc's eyebrows arched in surprise. "Do you want to forget Tessa exists?"

He stiffened then forced his fingers to unfurl. "No, never."

"Do you wish she was here, or you were there?"

The idea of it was so delicious Cam took a moment to savor it, how her face would light up with joy at seeing him. How she'd cuddle in his arms like she belonged there. "Yes, I shouldn't have let her leave."

"You did it to protect her. Noble of you but stupid." Marc chuckled, as if he found Cam's decision humorous.

He glowered at Marc, clasping his hands between his thighs to prevent him from punching his friend. Volatile emotions shuddered through him, and he struggled to calm them.

"Do you know if she's safe now?"

Cam nodded, not wanting to reveal he had Watts camping outside her home.

"Is she happy?"

A shrug rolled his shoulders, though he couldn't quite master an air of nonchalance.

"Good morning, sleepyhead, rise, and shine. So many things to see, too many women to do. Up you get, sweetheart. Time waits for no man, not even your sexy ass."

Cam jerked back, his chest seizing at hearing Tessa's voice. Roaring, he lunged across the couch to snatch Marc's phone. His friend leaped away, holding the phone above his head. Her sexy voice tore lust and love through Cam, shooting electricity along every nerve. He'd deleted the recording from his phone when he realized he'd become reliant on it to fall asleep.

He croaked before clearing his throat. "Marc...please."

"Go to her." Marc switched off his phone, but not before forwarding the recording to Cam, again.

He shook his head despite being grateful. "I can't."

"Liquidize everything, fake your death, and get your ass to South Africa."

Cam stilled, his breath hitching. Marc made it sound so simple, and he had considered it at one point. To be free of this life, to hand the reins over to Logan, to never have to kill another man, and to see Tessa again. All good things.

"Where would I start?" He slumped into the couch. "Will she want to see me?"

"There's only one way to find out. If she doesn't, you can seduce her with your special brand of charm."

Seduce her? His groin blazed at the imagery his memories replayed while his heart twanged with hope. "This is a silly idea, Marc. Faking a death isn't simple."

"I have one or two corpses lying around." Logan strode into the office.

"What are you doing here? And you promised not to kill anyone." Cam scowled.

"Heard you'd arrived. I have to tell you, I don't like being woken at this time of night." Logan's camel-colored chinos and blue T-shirt were crisp, but his hair was tousled, and a shadow darkened his jaw. "I have bodies left over from Dad's more...volatile days. A little dental rework, a car explosion, and you're dead."

Cam pinched and released his chin, considering Logan's offer. "Marc's the executor of my will, so he can handle my estate postmortem. I'll funnel an extra few million into my offshore accounts just in case."

"Mm, with you dead, your identity might be questioned, and your access denied. I suggest we transfer funds into an account created for Tessa." Logan leaned his ass on Cam's desk and folded his arms across his chest.

"No one would question that, and you can close your offshore accounts before your death."

Excitement hit Cam in the chest, spurring his heartbeat into overdrive. He jumped to his feet to pace the length of the room. "Am I doing this?" He grinned, letting it crack his stiff cheeks. "What name were you thinking?"

"Cameron to make it easier for you to respond to. Any last name will do." Marc hurried to the desk and picked up the phone, ready to order new identity documents.

"Choose a South African one." Cam laughed, his eagerness to see Tessa overwhelming his previous misery. He'd find her then tell the woman he bloody well loved her.

Pulling his phone from his back pocket, he flicked to the photos Watts's had sent him. A motorcyclist threw a leg over the back of the bike, removed the helmet, and Tessa's bronze locks tumbled free. There were shadows under her eyes like she couldn't sleep either, but the smile she wore was for her daughter, a taller replica of her.

Just like that, air left his chest as if siphoned out, and he met Marc's gaze. "Do it."

Chapter Twenty-One

MORE THAN A MONTH had passed, and still, Tessa couldn't get through the day without shedding a tear or two. Time was supposed to heal all wounds, yet no one knew how much time she needed. Her divorce had been amicable since she hadn't contested any of Forest's demands. What did it matter if he wanted half the furniture or half the proceeds from the sale of the house? He wasn't an unreasonable or unjust man, just a lying, cheating bastard. The spring cleaning had served as a distraction, and the house was show-ready.

Having never lived on her own before meeting Forest, she was looking forward to a quiet apartment, *her* dirty dishes in the sink, *her* mess in the lounge, and endless silence while she wrote her next novel. Something fun came to mind, a quirky and plump heroine who wrote romance and lived in a small town covered in snow.

She would have a man's name because her father had only wanted boys and had raised her and her brother as such. The hero would be her brother's best friend; a large, lumbering lumberjack or something requiring strength, and he was the new owner of a hunting lodge. She disapproved of killing for sport and was quite vocal about it, harassing the mayor, inciting the townsfolk, and causing quite a nuisance of herself.

It would be a new series; a romance writer writing about a romance writer. Maybe Tessa would call it Sensuous Scribblers? Wicked Wordsmiths? She bit her lip. Naming the series could wait until she had written a second one.

It had been a while since the muse had reared his fastidious head. The last time was when Cam had come home in a bloodied T-shirt. Forcing the memory aside in the hopes it didn't trigger fresh tears, she darted to her desk to type a synopsis. In an hour or so, the realtor would be by with the first few viewers. The market wasn't favorable toward sellers at present, but Tessa wanted this done. A little knock in the sale price meant a less fancy apartment, but waiting wasn't an option.

Her gate bell rang too soon, and she saved her document before hurrying to the front door. Drawing in a deep breath, she ran her sweaty palms down her high-waisted pencil skirt. The fabric was a kaleidoscope of colors to offset her broken heart. Her white shirt was crisp with a high collar, the blue gemstone and dragonfly necklace peeking out. She'd gathered her hair to the side and let it drape over one shoulder. Pink lipstick added color to her pale face, and a little concealer hid the shadows under her eyes. She'd gained weight too, unable to survive without drowning out her emotions. After she moved into an apartment, she'd return to her diet.

Sighing, she buzzed the realtor in, sight unseen, and opened her front door, pasting a bright smile on her lips. It faltered, trembled, then widened. No, she was imagining it. Sucking in a shuddering breath, she shook her head to dispel her overactive thoughts, and this time, when she raised her head, it was with dread.

She wanted Cam to be standing on her doorstep. What a fool she was.

"Tessa." The apparition's voice was just like Cam's.

She gasped and stumbled forward on her stilettoes. "You're real?"

The distance closed between them in an instant, and she was in his arms, not knowing who moved first. Her ears buzzed as her pounding heart rose to choke her. His cologne filled her nose, and she drank it in, tightening her arms around him. This wasn't real. She was dreaming. Hot joy and contentment softened her muscles, and she sighed.

"Did you miss me?" His rasping baritone summoned shivers, and she nodded, unable to speak. His body warmed her palms. She rested her cheek against solid muscle, and his hands gripped her hips like they used to.

"Yes." She squeezed his waist. If this was a dream, she could do and say anything without repercussions. "Why didn't you ask me to stay?" She pulled away to meet his gaze, struck anew by their blue depths. Cupping his cheeks, she brushed her lips across his, amazed at how her mind conjured the darts of desire, recalled the taste of him, and other gestures she hadn't noted in the heat of passion.

He didn't answer, except to kiss her again, diving in and taking control with a sweep of his tongue.

Unable to bear the torment, she groaned and pushed away. She was making progress and allowing herself these cherished daydreams with him centerstage would set her back. Her heart twanged at the loss of him anew, and she shuddered with unfulfilled desire.

"I can't...do this." She wrapped her arms around her waist, as if doing that would hold together the splintered remains of her heart. "I'm not strong enough to survive dreaming of you, Cam. Return to the ether, and let me rest."

"Um, Tessa-luv, you're not dreaming." He gestured to a man leaning against a black SUV. "That's Watts. I've had him tailing you since you left me."

"What?" She squeaked in dismay. So much for being aware of her surroundings. "But why? I texted you I was home." She squeaked. Ice drenched her face seconds before fire engulfed it. "You're here? This is real?" She squealed, throwing herself at him. He caught her with a laugh rumbling up from his belly, and it was music to her starved ears. "Cam." Tears spilled, and she buried her face where his shoulder met his neck. As happy as she was to see him, she couldn't understand why he stood before her. She inched back, just a little, to meet his gaze. "Why are you here?"

"South Africa's now my country, and if you'll let me, I'd like to call you my home."

She blinked. What was he saying? "You moved here?" She frowned. "I don't understand."

He chuckled and snatched a kiss. "I love you, Tessa."

She gasped, and a thousand suns exploded in her chest. "What...what did you say?"

He laughed and swept her into his arms. "I love you, sweet, adorable, sexy-as-hell Tessa."

"I...I love you too." She couldn't believe it. "Are you sure I'm not dreaming?"

He didn't answer except to kiss her, crushing her within his arms while he pinned his lips to hers, alternating between gentle flicks and deep, lust-inducing forays. "I hoped you loved me too," he whispered against her mouth.

She thumped him on the chest. "Why let me leave then? One word from you and I would've stayed."

"I didn't want you in danger, but I wasn't coping with you gone. Marc and Logan suggested this." He tugged his passport out of his jeans and showed it to her. "Cameron de Beer. Somewhere in England is a charred corpse matching my dental records, and for all intents and purposes, Camden Mathews is dead."

"Just like that?" She cupped his cheek, rubbing her thumb across his chin, not willing to address whose charred corpse he'd used. "What about your mother, sister, friends?"

"My family got a sizable inheritance, not as much though, as if I'd died for real. I thought I was close to Selena, but you saw how deceived I was. Logan and Marc are my only friends, and I doubt I've lost touch with them completely." Cam grinned and dipped his head to kiss her palm. "So, Tessa, will you marry me?"

Her emotions warred as she stared at him. Her first response was a resounding yes. She *was* a free, single woman. At his proposal, joy, hope, and love warmed her, swelled her lungs, and shot tingles of excitement through her. "I just finalized my divorce."

"I know." He smiled, tightening his arms around her. "We don't have to marry now, tomorrow is fine, next week will do, or maybe in a month if you convince me to wait. I want you in my arms always, in my bed every night, and in my life until my real death. I want your joy filling the darkness of my soul. I want your sexy accent to consume my ears. I want to bury myself in your delectable body, and your kisses to greet me coming or going. Please...Tessa, marry me."

Tears streamed down her cheeks again. She thought she was all cried out, hoped she was, but these were different tears stemming from joy and happiness.

"Yes." She kissed him, uncaring that she smeared her wet face against his.

He wiped her cheeks with the pads of his thumbs and grinned. "Right answer."

About the Author

Sevannah Storm is a fiction writer who immerses herself in fantastical worlds both magical and science fiction. She has a flare for the creative, having studied art and interior architecture, and spends her time drawing, oil painting, and writing. An avid reader from an early age, Sevannah finds her inspiration from various sources: games, novels, music, and the land of make-believe. The unique versus the practical has brought on numerous debates.

In her spare time, she does Pilates and rereads novels that snatch her breath away. Having embraced the social media world, you can find her on most platforms.

Her home is a land south of Wakanda, where animals roam free. Born in Zimbabwe, she grew up in South Africa. The crisp blue skies with cotton-candy sunsets expand her heart and soul, encapsulating a sense of freedom.

Words she lives by: "Know your pothole and dodge it. Don't work in a pencil factory if you're a vampire."

Sevannah loves to hear from her readers. You can find and connect with her at the links below.

Website/Newsletter:

https://www.sevannahstorm.com/

Facebook:

https://www.facebook.com/sevannah.storm

Instagram:

https://www.instagram.com/sevannah.storm/

Twitter:

https://twitter.com/sevannah_storm

Thank you for taking the time to read *Keeping Tessa*. If you enjoyed the story, please tell your friends and leave a review. Reviews support authors and ensure they continue to bring readers books to love and enjoy.